The Target Box

Ryan Scoville

FOR AMY

Thank you for always holding my hand.

PROLOGUE

I'm walking south along the Inner Drive. I'm drunk, wavering as I go, veering toward the sidewalk's edge and almost stumbling over a low-cut hedge before rebalancing. Luckily, the sidewalk is empty. The street is also empty. Some distant traffic on Lake Shore Drive dully swooshes by like the repetitive roil of waves on the beach. The sun will rise in a few hours. Chicago's quiet emptiness could probably be described as having a subdued, underwater feel, although nowadays I would describe everywhere as having an underwater feel. It seems to be a permanent condition.

I watch my footfalls as they pass through a slow rhythm of light and dark beneath the spread of overhead streetlamps. When I look up I see a man much farther down turn the corner towards me. He's big, older, and is led by a dog on a leash who is good sized, lean and vicious. He looks Eastern European or Russian, and I think he's the type of guy who, if you've been stuffed in a car trunk and taken for a long drive, is the first person you see when that trunk finally opens. The Russian looks like the type of guy who's seen things, done things, and is someone you don't want to mess with. He walks strangely askew, his left side slightly crumpled and weak while his right side, the one that holds the leash, looks like it could break down doors, break down about anything without much trouble. He looks like his two halves fought and there was a clear winner. He looks a moment away from uttering something in Russian, a staccato of consonants, and as you wonder what he said, the dog would be upon you.

As I walk from the darkness into the bluish tint of the next streetlight, he gets a good look at me and does an almost imperceptible twist of the wrist. The dog obeys and veers right, onto the street, away from me. There's no sidewalk on the other side so he walks down the middle of the street. He stares straight ahead, purposely avoiding eye contact. He doesn't want anything to do with me. Most people would make the same choice because of what I'm carrying, the way I'm weaving with each step. I'm guessing the Russian knows a thing or two and knows not to tangle with someone who has nothing to lose. Not that he's afraid of me, not even close, but there's nothing to gain, only loss.

I smile to myself, laughing that this Russian mobster, the one I imagine to be an enforcer, steers clear of me rather than the other way around. Though I'm of average build, a runner's build, a build that wouldn't be much trouble for the Russian or his dog, he knows there are more reasons to avoid a man than his size. For starters, my clothes have dried vomit on them. A polo, nice pressed khakis and sandals, well put together and quite stylish at one point, are now merely a canvas for my self-inflicted retching. It's my vomit, but it's not my fault, not really. I was actually doing pretty well this year, all things considered, and wasn't too drunk. Earlier today, or I guess yesterday evening, I found myself in some restaurant sitting with a group of eight: three guys and five girls, cozying up with the one named Teagan. We met the day before and I actually liked her, so to speak. I couldn't truly like someone, wouldn't let it get beyond a hand on the back as we walked through the door, a brush of fingers along her arm while someone made a joke, but I liked the idea of liking her, and that was enough. She covered her mouth when she laughed. She offered words of encouragement to her friends for no reason whatsoever. And she wore a bracelet with live flowers woven into it. I asked her about the bracelet, holding her hand while inhaling the sweet perfume of wildflowers wrapped in a strand of baby's breath, and she admitted that once they died, she plucked them out and wove in new flowers. I think this final trait, this hopeful innocence, is why I liked her so much while simultaneously being the reason it would never work out.

I had been a perfect gentleman the whole day, making small talk with her friends as we watched the Cubs game, and actually thought I might make it through the weekend in one piece as we all taxied to some Old Town restaurant they all raved about. The restaurant's claim to fame was in perfecting classic comfort foods: chicken pot pie with locally grown leeks, corn bread served in a cast iron skillet, infused with bacon and topped with a sweet orange marmalade; grilled cheese sandwiches with gorgonzola and aged cheddar cheeses beneath a sun-dried tomato and garlic-thyme aioli, topped with a cool dollop of chive butter. They loaded up the fat, added uncommon ingredients, and tried to stamp their signature onto these cuisine staples. We ordered some of everything and passed them around, so I never thought about it when a mini-cocotte filled with macaroni and cheese came around. I put some on my plate and began eating, barely noticing the crescent moon slices of meat, assuming they were some exotic sausage. I finally considered what it could be and asked around. Nobody knew for sure, but somebody blurted out that it, "Looks like bits of hot dog."

I froze, alarms going off, refusing to chew or swallow another bite as I carefully spit a mouthful into my napkin. I'm not allergic to hot dogs, but could hardly breathe knowing I had swallowed pieces cut so small I barely noticed them. I flagged down our waitress and whispered a request for nine shots of vodka. I sat patiently, no longer able to hear the conversations going on around me, just catching the echoes of laughter. There were protestations as the waitress returned with nine shots on her tray, but I ignored them and instructed her to place them before me, everyone expecting me to hand them out. Teagan said something about having to work the next day. I nodded, knowing I would never see her again, and then poured all nine shots into my empty water glass. The table went quiet, eyebrows curled as the friends furtively glanced at each other, wondering what this stranger recently introduced into their group was about to do. Each watched, hoping someone else would intervene, but nobody did anything as I lifted the glass and began to chug. It was supposed to burn, but I could barely feel it, only sensing that rot in my stomach of descending hot dog turning and tumbling before reversing course. I stood up and only felt relief as I began vomiting. I refused to lean forward, refused to blow it outward, and instead looked up as it poured out my mouth and ran down my shirt and shorts, landing on my sandaled feet. My stomach muscles finally unclenched, and I caught my breath as the whole restaurant stared, Teagan's friends with mouths agape, and Teagan recoiling that she had just been holding hands with me. I pulled a hundred dollar bill out of my pocket, laid it on the table and whispered something incomprehensible before walking out the door.

That was so many hours ago, so many beers and so many bars ago, but the stench is still there. Of course, the Russian wouldn't just avoid a drunk who threw up on himself. He's also probably suspicious that I'm carrying a shovel in one hand. It's not quite full size, but it's a weapon nonetheless. And you seldom see someone carrying a shovel through the paved city, let alone an hour before sunrise on a Monday morning. In my other hand, curled against my side, is a small wooden box with a pattern of hash marks engraved on the lid. I don't have the key, which is fine, since I won't ever open it. So I can't blame the Russian for avoiding the drunk covered in vomit carrying a shovel and a wooden box. I can't blame him for avoiding me.

I purse my lips to smile at this thought and taste salt. I press the back of my hand into my mouth and see red across my thumb. My mouth's bleeding. My mouth's bleeding, and that's another reason to avoid me. I can explain the vomit, the shovel and the box, but I don't know why my mouth's bleeding. The last eight hours have been a blur of binge drinking, eventually finding myself in a park with a bottle of vodka after closing time.

I turn to the Russian as he passes on the street and shout, "My mouth's bleeding! Hey Bert, my mouth's bleeding!"

He doesn't look my way, doesn't flinch, following the straight line down the center of the street. I guess his name's not Bert, but that won't stop me. "Zuzu's petals!" I shout. "Zuzu's petals!" I put my hands in my pockets and search around, and for a tiny thread of time it's not an act. I hope to find Zuzu's petals. The only way any of this could make sense is if I find Zuzu's petals in my pocket. My pinched fingers come out with some crumpled bills and a ticket stub, which I drop to the sidewalk.

It's a Wonderful Life? Really? Fuck you, Jimmy Stewart. Fuck you, Frank Capra. And fuck you, Clarence. But as I think of Clarence, the angel who saved George Bailey, I get an idea, a new plan, and I like it. I turn off inner Lake Shore at Division and head west, then back south on State Street. I'm still wavering as I walk but I'm determined, and when I pass a construction site cordoned off, I rip off a section of tape and jam it in my pocket. As I pass the condos and apartment buildings, I shout out, "Merry Christmas, movie house! Merry Christmas, emporium! Merry Christmas you wonderful old Savings and Loan!" It's August, the hot part of August, and shouting Merry Christmas seems like the perfect thing to do.

When I eventually find my way to the State Street Bridge, I make my way to the very middle. The Chicago River winds its way below through the canyon of skyscrapers, and a soft light from the impending sunrise fills the void. It's beautiful, a pause of pure splendor before the ugly snarl of Monday morning. I take the construction tape out of my pocket and wrap the box up on one end, securing it with a standard knot. On the other end I tie the shovel, leaving a few inches of slack between them. I lean over the railing holding the shovel and box outstretched and look around, searching for Clarence. I am honestly hopeful that an angel will jump into the river and try to save me, but it never happens. Instead, with a great thrust, I launch them over the railing and into the river below.

I can't see them fall, but hear the plunge as the shovel and the Target box hit the water. I step away from the railing and exhale. Another year.

"What the hell're you doing?" shouts a figure emerging from the south end of the bridge. I wait for him to approach, his outline forming into one of Chicago's finest.

"I don't know."

"What the hell did you throw over the bridge?"

"It was just a small box."

"A box? What was in it?"

"I don't know."

"Bullshit! You know I can get divers down there."

"Divers for a small box? That's fine, but it'll be a waste of time."

"So you know what was in the box?"

"No, but there's nothing illegal. It's not like it was drugs or anything."

"Then what was it?"

"I really don't know." I may get arrested. Minimally I'll get a ticket for public intoxication, perhaps littering or something like that. I don't care.

"Where are you going now?" the policeman asks.

"Back to my hotel. The W."

"And after that?"

"After I sleep this off? I'm going to shower, check out and drive home."

"Where's home?"

"Athens, Georgia."

The policeman ponders this, knowing every minute with me is a minute more likely someone will walk by, a minute more likely he'll have to do his job and arrest me.

"Dammit," he finally says. "Go and get the fuck out of here."

"Yes, sir," I say, and take his advice by heading south.

"And don't come back to Chicago," he says.

"Yes, sir," I lie.

Ryan Scoville

One Year Later

THE P'S – PART I

My father was a minister and my mother was a physics professor. I'm finally writing it down.

Almost twenty years ago Mr. Keller, my high school English teacher, told me that sentence was the perfect start to a story. He was that one teacher who, after a lifetime of teaching the same kids through the system, watching us make the same mistakes and turning into the same shallow, lost adults, continued to believe every student was important and hoped to make a difference in each of our lives. Because of this, he was made fun of by the faculty almost as much as by the students. In retrospect, I guess I admired his blind optimism over the other teachers who were picking out failures and treating them as such from day one, even if they were right.

My freshman year, Mr. Keller had us write an autobiographical paper, to which I complained that I had nothing to write about. He then asked me a litany of questions: Did I play any sports? Did I have any pets? What did I do over summer vacation? What did my parents do? As soon as I told him my father was a minister and my mother was a physics professor, his face lit up. He grabbed me by the shoulders and said, "There. That's where you start your story." I had no idea what he was talking about.

He was so excited. I could tell he wished his parents were such an interesting mix, imagining an endless supply of short stories he could send off to literary magazines as a man of the cloth and a woman of the molecule traveled together through life. How fascinating would it be to watch two people, whose interests in life were such polar opposites, decide to unite as a family?

He didn't even know that my mother was a staunch atheist, confident that things began with a bang, followed by a few billion years of evolution, and eventually culminating into the self-evident anarchy we have today. She was confident that once her time was up, that was it, the big nothing. Of course she still attended my father's church, but in her mind it was more out of duty, like a professional football player's wife sitting in the stands even though she has no interest in the game. She didn't tell other members of the congregation either. In fact, she was known for asking the tough questions about religion, offering them up with a curious smile and letting people struggle to find an answer. They assumed she knew the answers, and by making them struggle she was helping them strengthen their faith. In reality these were the questions that led her to believe all of Christianity was a lot of foolish people trying to put meaning to the meaningless.

My mom's career choice was easy to comprehend. She never liked people and was good with numbers. As a result she got a master's degree in both mathematics and physics, discovering that if she was an expert in these fields, people would accept her social awkwardness and attitude of general disdain when dealing with everyday people, whom she called, "people of a lesser intellect." My father also harbored contempt for people as a whole, but sadly for him as well as the thousands of parishioners that attended Faith Church, he wasn't good with numbers. Instead he had a photographic memory and a knack for quoting scripture, discovering its uncanny ability to drive people away, especially those he described as "people of a lesser faith."

But for me, they didn't have to discuss Calabi-Yau Manifolds or Job as a Messianic Apologetic to drive me away. I knew to keep quiet early on, to keep my goo-goos and gaa-gaas to myself. "He was a quiet baby," they said. And being told I was a quiet baby only made it seem natural to become a quiet boy, and eventually a quiet man. At least around them.

In truth, I seldom heard them argue about their beliefs. In truth, I seldom heard them talk. They allowed each other to believe what they wanted. My father submitted to a higher power, while my mother submitted to no power. And since they respected each other's beliefs, I accepted that somehow God and anarchy could coexist in life, just as they did in my house. At my father's funeral, when I stood over the casket containing a man who had suffered interminably from intestinal cancer that eventually ate into his spine, causing blindness and paralysis, I grasped his folded hands and thought, "Now you know." At my mother's memorial service, after a brain aneurysm unexpectedly took her in the middle of the night, I lay my hand on the urn and thought, "Now you don't."

I accepted both of their world views and instead concentrated my beliefs on the only thing I could see around me: I believed in people. When I could get out of the house, I hung out with friends, went to parties, and basically ignored anything and everything about my home life. My friends and I would cause as much trouble as we could without getting into serious trouble. My social life was the only thing important to me, and once I moved out on my own, once my parents passed away, it was the only thing I had to worry about.

Mr. Keller thought my parents were a fascinating mix because he was sure there were interesting stories to tell. I'm sure he was also curious as to what type of child would come out of that household. In hearing the constant battle between the atom and Adam, who would win, what view of the world would he have? As it turned out, this was a question I would spend my whole life ignoring. But as it turned out, I couldn't ignore it forever.

THE P'S – PART II

THE NAME GAME

I've been driving for a little over eight hours, up from Athens, Georgia into Illinois. It's another four or five hours to Chicago, and I'm going to save that for tomorrow. It's just after 7:00 on a humid Thursday night, and it's about time to wet my whistle.

I packed this morning, overpacked, because it was just a matter of throwing things into bags and then the trunk. Shorts and polos, a Cubs jersey, a few nice outfits just in case, a few pairs of shoes and my dopp kit. Plus the Target Box, nestled between my suitcase and the duffel bag with my running gear. As soon as I got on the highway, I rolled down the windows, turned up the volume and pushed in the tape, The Best of OMD, which came out over thirty years ago. I'm old, but right now I don't know it. Right now I feel young. Eventually I run out of cassettes and pull out some contraption that plugs into the audio port on my phone and hooks up to a fake tape cassette, allowing me to play songs from my collection. This is the stuff I listen to when I run: Metallica, Iron Maiden, G n' R and the Crüe. I'm old, but the Mustang has a V8 that hums, just waiting for me to shake the reins and tell her to go. She's got speakers in the back that match her engine, able to blare loud enough that no one could ever enjoy it in the car, and only meant to make the ground shake with her bass as she pulls up to make a scene. I don't turn the volume all the way up, except for "Master of Puppets." For eight minutes I bang my head to Master and put the speedometer over a hundred along some Tennessee highway.

It's not all metal. "Life is a Highway" plays a few times. It seems appropriate on a road trip, no matter how much I disagree with the title. It's just a song so I let it do its job and take me somewhere. It's been a year since I had a sip of alcohol, and I haven't wanted any since then, but I know I'm having some tonight, just a bit to start the weekend, and I'm excited. I have to admit it. Alcohol can put me in a better mood before the first sip, just knowing it's a drinking day, just knowing I've taken care of everything else and have nothing else to do besides tie one on, tomorrow be damned. I feel like I've earned it, and it does not matter whether that is true or not.

I eat lunch and dinner on the road, and follow my GPS off the highway and into Carbondale, home of Southern Illinois University, making my way to the hotel most parents stay at when visiting. School is a week from starting, so the town is empty, but the hotel bar is one kids don't hang out at anyway, at least according to the web. I park in front, get out and stretch, turning from side to side, touching my toes, reaching over head. It feels good, but there's no breeze and it's hot outside. I open the trunk, grab my bags and stare at the Target Box, alone in the trunk. I rest my hand on the soft wood, grasp the lock in front and give it a slight pull. I clutch it under my arm and go to the hotel and check in under the relief of air conditioning. Once in my room on the fourth floor, I wash my face, stretch a little more, check the mirror to make sure nothing is out of sorts, and leave my room, eyeing the Target Box sitting out on the dresser as the door clicks shut. I step down the carpeted hallway to the elevator, feeling light on my feet.

Surprisingly, the hotel bar is pretty nice. It's very nice, especially for a college town, which must be why this is where parents stay when visiting. It's called The Matchbox, and there's a large fireplace just past the entrance, encircled with high-backed leather chairs. It's too hot to even think of a fire, and the chairs are empty. In the middle is a large rectangular bar, made of dark woods underlined by brass foot rails, and it couldn't be any better for my exploits. Around the bar is a two-tiered dining room, the first-level filled with round, open tables and the second with cozy, two-person tables and tall booths, for those who prefer to be tucked away. I make a half-lap around the bar and perch myself on the corner farthest from the door, careful not to look around as I sit, knowing the locals are looking at me.

The bartender, not doing anything but cleaning glasses that are already clean, lets a few minutes pass before acknowledging me, making sure I understand the pace of things while he's on duty. He finally comes over, dries his hands on a towel, and raises an eyebrow to let me know he is ready. I can tell he doesn't like me, which is just fine, as I couldn't really care less about him except I want a drink. So fuck him. I hold up a finger for him to wait, studying the scotches grouped together on a mirrored shelf, and I order the one I don't see, a Glenfiddich. Without pause the bartender disappears around the island of liquors and walks back with a half-full bottle. "Neat?" he asks.

Even with the air conditioner blaring, I know it's hot outside, and it's been a year since I've had a drink. I want it cool and easy to sip. "On the rocks. Lot of 'em."

For a small college town in southern Illinois, I can't say how impressed I am with The Matchbox. Most bars along this route only serve Budweiser, only have a few barstools that are filled by the locals, and make me feel like

I'm crazy when I do what I'm about to do.

The bartender goes back to his glass-cleaning ritual, and I let my scotch dilute while I pull out a leather-bound journal that looks as if it had accompanied me through the African Sahara or up the Amazon Basin. In reality, it's had that look since the day I bought it, at a Hallmark store, shelved between ceramic animal figurines and the Hello Kitty cards. I open it to the first blank page and begin to slowly write the date, watching the loops and turns along the path of a cursive *August*.

After the date, I give the glass a swirl and take a long inhale. The glass is cold in my hand, but the smell is hot and peaty. I tilt it to my lips, just enough to wet them, and can feel the burn. That's enough for now. I'm only having two drinks tonight, as I want to feel fresh tomorrow. Tomorrow's really the start to my weekend and this is just a teaser. Nothing's happening tonight except for me acting like a pretentious ass.

My handwriting is atrocious, a doctor's penmanship, but I can get it halfway legible if I write slowly and tighten my grip. And so I practice, writing:

'Twas brillig, and the slithy toves
Did gyre and gimble in the wabe:

The Jabberwocky. I don't remember the rest of the poem, just two lines of senseless words that combine into senseless beats that for some reason, I think make sense. I won't write anything serious here; can't. If I were to write anything real, I would need real quiet, a place away from the world, tucked away and timeless, like the alcove I once had next to my bed in the city. But not here. Instead, I just work on my handwriting, jotting down garbled phrases and nonsensical words, taking moments to sniff and sip my scotch, waiting. But even though the words I write aren't going anywhere, I find my mind does have the room to wander, to frolic around words that touch on meaning.

Watch the steady hand.
The lilting lilacs on Larrabee.
"And I, you."

I make notes but they hardly make sense. As I turn the page I know I'll never go back and read these scribblings. At best, I'll flip through the pages like a picture book and pretend there is something profound hidden within the meaningless scribble.

Eventually I pause and look around. A group of young men sit in a corner, drinking their beer while silently peeling off the labels. A few couples are scattered here and there. At one table sits a group of women, a little younger than me, and I make eye contact with the one looking at me. She smiles and I smile back with a slight nod, keeping eye contact until she looks for her glass of wine, gives it a twirl, and drinks. I go back to my writing and wait.

Eventually there is some movement next to me, and when I look up, there is the same girl, her thumb and forefinger clutching the stem of her wine glass. She offers another smile and a "Hi."

"Hello," I say, laying my pen into the nest of the open book's spine.

"What are you writing?"

"Oh, not much. Just scribbling down some ideas."

"Are you a writer?"

Now that deserves a pause, which I give to her as if I'm thinking, although I know the answer. "No, I write, used to write a lot, but I'm not a writer." And I'm quite sure of this, having proven it before. There's another pause and I introduce myself.

"I'm Paige," she returns.

Paige looks to be in her mid-thirties, my age. She has a heart-shaped face with a thin nose atop a thin, athletic body. But her speckled brown hair stands out in waves, running across her forehead, jumping out from behind her ears and playing along her solid white shirt. She has a lot of hair, if only because there is so little to the rest of her. She is also tan, a slightly aged darkness that she clearly spends time trying to achieve. And although her tan has caused premature wrinkles, I find it attractive, as if her weathered look means a weathered life. So at least we'll have something to talk about.

She's wearing jeans and a bleach-white button up, with most of the top buttons undone. The shirt manages to hold itself close together, not revealing too much, but expressing possibilities. I'm definitely attracted to Paige, except for the whiff of cigarette smoke she brought with her. I don't think she smokes, but her friends are working hard on their smoke signals at the other end of the bar. I don't care much, though. Cigarette smoke can layer nicely with the scent of a peaty scotch. She turns away and inhales her wine, then lifts it and drinks, and I can see just inside her shirt, revealing the tendons from her neck holding out like bridge cables. They're not grotesque, probably not abnormal, but there's something about them I don't like. They pull outward like tree roots protruding from the dirt, the kind little boys trip over when they play.

That's a minor thing though. Paige is attractive and she has a lovely, confessional smile, and that's good enough.

Hmm, Paige. Let's play the name game, Paige.

Paige. Paige. Paige. The letter P it is.

Puh… Puh… Place?

"So Paige, are you from Exeter?"

"Practically. I'm from Murphysboro."

"Murphysboro?"

"Yeah, it's just up the road. And you?"

"I live in Athens, Georgia. I'm just passing through."

"Georgia? Where's your drawl?"

"I lived most of my life in Illinois, in and around Chicago, so no drawl for me. You'll hear me say 'pop' instead of 'soda,' although they really don't say 'soda' because I swear everything down there's a Coke."

Paige laughs and hopefully now I'm a bit worldly and wise. Time to keep the name game going. Paige. Paige. Paige. Profession? The name game was just something that came out of being single downtown. McCarron used to always say how, when you first met a girl, you had to keep talking. It didn't matter what you said as long as you kept talking. Everything out of McCarron's mouth came across as funny, confident, and always a bit flirtatious with the ladies, but it's true the guy could just keep talking and talking.

"So Paige, what do you do for a living?"

"I'm a sales consultant."

"What type of sales?"

"Pharmaceuticals."

"So you call on doctors?"

"Sort of. I'm inside sales. It's more tracking and fulfillment for our outside sales team. Inside sales is just a fancy term for managing orders. Getting things where they need to be."

"So you do logistics?"

"Yes. Logistics is probably a better term."

"Sometimes I feel like all of life is logistics."

Paige nods. "I have to agree with you there. So if you're not a writer, what do you do?"

"I'm a psychologist." I realize that counts for a P too. Really, the name game was all about asking questions, but we like to use it for answers too. McCarron would introduce the girl he met at the end of the bar and say – This is Patti, I call her Patti Melt, and though she's never been to Princeton, she has been to Paris, loves pandas and Pegasus ponies, and has purple peonies growing in her garden. And Pattie would give him a look of wonder while we'd all laugh. But it worked, as long as you kept talking. So Paige is in pharmaceutical sales while I'm a psychologist, and though neither has the P sound, I'm counting them.

"Really? That has to be interesting. What type of people do you deal with?"

"I work at a clinic that's, well, it's more of a resort than a medical facility. A quiet little resort surrounded by soy fields and peach trees, where we help people who just need a break from, well, anything and everything: depression, anxiety eating disorders, various compulsions and drug abuse.

Lots of drug abuse, but we have all sorts."

"Very interesting."

"Yeah, I guess."

"More interesting than inside sales."

"Logistics, you mean. I do logistics too."

"How so?" Paige asks.

I sip my scotch, just enough to coat my lips and tongue, and enough to make Paige wait. "I try to get things where they need to be, same as you. Maybe not physical things, but it's all logistics."

"You help people."

"I guess. I try to." At work. But only at work.

"It sounds more exciting than sitting on the phone all day and making sure people's orders are correct."

"People are interesting, I'll give you that, but I work with people going through tough times. Every one of them has a reason, a breaking point, for eventually ending up there, and they don't feel like they have a way forward, that at best life will be a slogging through, and at worst, things are just going to get worse. It's generally not the sunniest of work environments."

Paige pauses, probably contemplating drug addiction, debilitating depression and suicidal tendencies, or at least that's what I contemplate, and I realize I'm bringing things down. Time to move on. Paige, P, puh-puh-puh-Paris.

"Have you ever been to Paris?" I distinctly remember one time McCarron was talking to a girl named T-something, Theresa I think, and all of a sudden tells her he just got a new toaster and would she like to see it. And just like that, they were outside hailing a cab back to his place to see an appliance for toasting bread. We were cocky assholes, there's no doubt about that. But really, what are you supposed to talk to a stranger about? We were trying to flirt, and the whole Catch-22 is that the best way to flirt is not acting like you're flirting. So toasters for Theresa and Pegasus ponies for Patti were what we came up with. We were assholes, but it didn't matter.

"Paris? Why do you ask?"

"You seem to know your wine. The proper swirl of the glass, an inhale before drinking, just wondering if you've ever been to the center of it all?"

"Oh no. I've never left the states."

"You'd love it. Especially if you like Cabs, the Bordeaux region is amazing."

"You've been?"

"Only once, but it was beautiful. Two days in Bordeaux, and the best red wine I've ever had. That's why I'm drinking scotch. It's hard to get anything that compares." I guess I'm trying to sound sophisticated, but I'm probably coming across as a world-class snob. Heck, most of the French wines described as "earthy" had too much in common with a barnyard floor. "What about California? Their wines can be just as good."

"No," Paige says, swirling her wine glass a little longer and taking a deeper inhale, not knowing that the bottle has probably been open behind the bar all week. Yes, I can be a snob. "I went to L.A. once, to visit a friend, but that's it."

"Oh no. L.A. is a world unto itself. Wine country is really nice there. I would recommend staying away from the main tourist destinations like Napa and Sonoma."

"How come?"

"Actually, I take that back. For your first visit they're perfect, but after that it's worth taking the road less traveled." I think for a moment, puckering my lips while trying to think of California locations. "You should try somewhere like Paso Robles or Petaluma, Paige." I doubt I could pick them out on a map, let alone say anything about their wines, but that's two points nonetheless. I finish my scotch and order a second. Whistle properly wetted; this will be my last one.

So far I've been a wuss with the name game. Asking "Place" and "Profession" is just another way of asking the two most common pickup lines, where are you from and what do you do. Paris, Paso Robles and Petaluma at least showed a little hustle and creativity.

Paige. Puh, puh... poinsettia... placebo... Pollyanna... political... politics. That'll do, politics.

"So, just getting to know you, what are your politics, Republican or Democrat?"

Wrong question. Paige looks at me uninterested. I should have known.

"I don't really follow that sort of stuff. So I'm neither or, what do you call it?"

"Atheist?" I offer, smiling into my drink. "Me too, depending on my options."

"No, that's not it."

"Apolitical?"

"Maybe that's it."

"What you mean is you've got better things to do."

"I say that, but I just think politics is so uninteresting. I was raised Republican, but most of my friends are Democrats, and I just found you can't trust anybody when it comes to politics."

"Smart girl," I concede. Time to change the subject. Paige. Puh, puh, puh. Pontification. Peter Piper Picked a Peck of Prideful Peppers... Pride. Yes, pride is perfect.

"So Paige, tell me something you're proud of."

She looks at me quizzically.

"No wait," I add, "tell me the thing that you're most proud of." This is a dangerous question, but there's plenty of upside. If she answers honestly, I'll know something real about her, something important, and we may have something to talk about for a while, but Paige continues to look at me quizzically. "I'm just trying to get to know you better."

"That's a tough one. How about we get to know you better first. What are you most proud of?"

And there's the problem with asking tough questions during the Name Game: you tend to get tough questions thrown back at you. This doesn't happen if you talk about toasters, but that's all right, I can lie. "Hmm, the thing I'm most proud of. Let's see." I look at her, preparing the lie.

"I'm not a writer, but I did write a book."

"Really?" she asks excitedly. I'm reeling her back in.

The lie is not that I wrote a book. I did. The lie is that it is the thing I'm most proud of. I was proud of it, once, but not anymore. And if I were proud of the book, the very highest it could make it on my list of accomplishments is third, as first and second are clearly taken.

"Yes. I mean, it wasn't that good. I'm just proud to have done it."

"So you are a writer. What was it about?"

"No, no, it's your turn now. What's the one thing you've done that you're most proud of?"

Paige squints her eyes and nervously pinches her left shirt cuff between her right index finger and thumb. The table of women she was sitting with keeps looking over, wondering what we're talking about. I ignore them and swivel towards Paige, ensuring our conversation is close and intimate.

"Okay, I've got it," she says with a smile she can't hold back, a new excitement that makes her momentarily look a decade younger. She looks like she may giggle.

"Let's hear it."

"Promise you won't laugh."

I touch the top of her hand, turn my head, and say in earnest, "Promise."

"I won the Spirit award on our cheerleading team. I also won Most Improved, but I'm most proud of the Spirit award."

"Really?"

"I never did much of anything in high school, but for some reason I tried out for the basketball cheerleading squad my junior year and made it. And I won those awards at the end of the season. Most spirit and most improved. I'd never won anything like that before."

"Wow. Awesome," I say. I'm surprised though. Paige doesn't seem like the most spirit type of girl. In fact, spending her Thursday night in a small town bar, drinking cheap wine with a group of chain smokers, she's the last person I'd pin most spirit on. "So you'd never done cheerleading before?"

"No, never."

"What about dance?"

"Nothing. I mean, I danced to the radio in my bedroom, but what teenage girl doesn't do that. I'd never even thought about it, didn't like school, thought most of the girls on the squad were stuck up bimbos even though I didn't know them."

"So what changed?"

"I dunno. I broke up with the guy I had been seeing, who would have laughed at me if I tried out for cheerleading."

"Laughed at you? I thought every guy wanted to date a cheerleader?"

"He was an ass. I was a freshman and he was a senior when we started dating. The next year, after he graduated, he wouldn't attend anything school related, like dances or football games, because he said he was too old for that and it was embarrassing. Yet somehow he managed to show up in the school parking lot at the end of the day and hang out once or twice a week. He was a loser, I was just too young to know it. When I finally figured it out and broke up with him, Miss Serbak, the cheerleading coach, asked me to try out. I had never even thought about it, but figured, 'Why not?'"

I look at her intently, with a growing smile.

"What?" Paige asks, self-conscious.

"You grew pretty."

She blushes, knowing exactly what I'm talking about. "What?"

"Just taking a guess here, but I imagine you were, uh, blossoming into a beautiful young woman, the cheerleading coach noticed, and that's why she told you to try out."

Confirming my guess, Paige coyly says, "Maybe."

"And it sounds like you wowed them all, Miss Spirit."

"Yeah, I really got into it for some reason. It sounds so dumb, but it was fun."

"That's great. How did you do your senior year?"

And that was the question that deflated the girl before me, sending her from a pom-pom twirling, legs-kicking, most-spirited high-school cheerleader, to the woman who needs another drink as she realizes it's twenty years later and she's talking to some stranger at a bar. "I didn't try out my senior year."

I don't want to press the issue, but it will look like I don't care if I leave it there. "How come?"

"Things came up," she says, which is good enough for me. We both sit in silence, thinking.

"So tell me more about your book," she says, changing the subject from one she doesn't want to talk about to one I don't want to talk about.

So what do I say? That after college I was vain enough to take a year off and write, vain enough to believe that with little practice or training I could

23

sit down at the age of twenty-two and rip out an American masterpiece? That I then wrote a book with cliché characters who delivered predictable movie lines to each other while pursuing one-dimensional goals, allowing everything to unfold in a predictable manner?

Margaret always said I was too down on myself, and she was right. I was once very proud of the book. I spoke highly of it, proudly, and wrote superlative-laden query letters and flowing synopses to many publishers. When that didn't go anywhere, I paid a vanity house to print it anyway, enough copies that I could hold one up and say, "I've been published." I wistfully store this experience under the guise of youth. Not only do I no longer write, I no longer dream of writing. But I am willing to dig out an old copy and use it as a prop, if it serves a purpose. Sorry, Margaret.

I reach into my bag and pull out a simple, black paperback with the words *The Gothic Century* printed across the cover. It kills me every time that the title is printed in a font called 'Trajan', considering the title comes from a specific font name, 'Century Gothic'. Just more proof that the publishing house I paid to print my book never actually read it, or at least never made it to page twenty-three, where the title is explained. As excited as I was to receive a copy, the physical book with the incorrect font confirmed I was paying to publish for my own pride. Paying to Publish for Pride. Damn name game, I think I scored on my own goal.

Paige is impressed nonetheless.

It's thick, it's bound, and it has my name on it. She can hold it in her hands, flip through the pages, and assume that all those words mean something, something of importance. "It was put out by a small publishing house," I say, "not a national bestseller or anything."

"This is so impressive," Paige says. "Can I show my friends?" I nod. She takes the book and heads over to her table of friends. They pass it around, turning it in their hands as if it were a newly discovered artifact, unsure which side is up. One of the girls opens it and reads a few pages in the middle. I can see her lips move, although I'm not sure if it's the way she reads or if she is reading a passage to the whole table. I hope it's not the ten-page diatribe on bull markets. Or the chapter called Pizzazz. Or any love scene.

How I wish I could put a lock on that book; it's so much better unopened.

Instead, I sit on my barstool and hold my posture, drink my drink and nod at them in acknowledgement. I am a writer in their presence, and I won't challenge that perception.

Paige brings my book back, saying, "This is amazing." She sits next to me again, this time facing me so that the inside of her knee is touching mine. Her hand brushes down my arm as she lays the book in front of me, and suddenly there is little space between us and we hold a comfortable proximity.

I should probably admit right now that I am attractive. Not insanely attractive, but just enough to have a woman like Paige come up and sit next to me without me ever making any advance toward her. It started occurring in my mid-twenties and every time a girl chooses to talk to me over someone else, I have to stop and think how funny it is, how I could be a complete idiot or a complete ass and I'd still have a hundred times more luck than the guy with the chubby jaw line, the receding hair line, or the yellow teeth. They say men are shallow, but they're only half-right. People are shallow.

But who am I to complain? We pretend there's some skill in the name game, some trick to keep the conversation going, but if you look good and act cool, a discussion on the merits of duct tape or the flavor profile of plain yogurt are suddenly a lot more palatable.

And so Paige and I continue our small talk. She takes me through her job, touching on sales reps, distribution channels, why she likes it, why she doesn't, etc., etc., while the only thing I notice is the way she leans her head sideways and runs her fingertips along my forearm. I tell her a little about the psychiatric hospital, about the dilapidated white barn outside the craft room window, standing idly on a hillside, and how most patients end up painting that scene at one time or another. It's for relaxation, I tell her, as we relax into a mix of each other's booze and breath.

"So why are you going to Chicago?" she asks.

"Just for a weekend getaway. I used to live there and sometimes like to visit."

"Are you meeting old friends?"

"No. I really haven't told anyone I'm coming. I'm not a good planner. The Cubs are playing in town, so I may try to catch a game."

"Against the Cardinals."

"Yeah, I think they are playing the Cards."

"Sounds fun."

"I hope so."

"I hate traveling alone though."

"Me too."

There's a long pause, and I immediately regret how I fill it, "I'm also bringing the Target Box."

"What's that?"

"The Target Box. It's a wooden box, about yay big, like a shoebox but a little taller, made of wood with leather bound straps, and a lock in the front. It's sitting in my hotel room." I like having a mystery, but I don't particularly like talking about the Target Box. I don't like putting it into words, defining it.

"I bet you can guess my next question."

"What's in it?"

"Yes, what's in it?"

"Nothing," I start, "I'm not sure."

"You don't know what's in it?"

This is why I regret bringing it up. A little mystery is good, too much mystery makes me sound like a douche. Or a drug dealer. "It's nothing really, just more of a tradition to bring it with me. Not a big deal."

"A tradition?"

"A long story."

It's late and the bar probably won't be open much longer, but Paige looks at her watch and then back at me, eyebrows raised, indicating she has all the time in the world.

"I don't really like to get into it."

"Then you shouldn't have brought it up."

"Tell me about it."

Paige proffers a laugh. "Do you do anything with this Target Box, or just bring it along?"

"No, nothing big. It's probably just a silly tradition that gives me a reason to return to Chicago, have some fun. Walk along the lakefront, do some shopping, eat at a few nice restaurants, visit a museum and possibly catch a Cubs game. It's pretty open ended, but that's what I'm doing this weekend. When was the last time you went to Chicago?"

"It's been years. At least five or six. Probably more."

"See, it's good to have a reason to go back."

"I guess so. I usually go to St. Louis to get away."

"You're comparing St. Louis to Chicago?"

"I know," Paige says, "but it's closer."

And we're off the subject. We chat some more, a little about her work, a little about mine, but mainly about stuff that isn't important at all. Paige has two more drinks and instead of limiting myself to two, I order a third scotch. The dickhead bartender is giving small pours, and it doesn't matter anyway; I'm just going to my room. Paige and I are close, to the point that if I were younger I would ask her for her number, but I yawn instead. She says in a manner that is flirtatious because it is so direct, "Why don't you show me that Target Box?"

I pause. To Paige, the Target Box might as well be a toaster oven, but I'm a little taken aback because it's important to me; it is not just an excuse to get her to my room. I call over the bartender and pay the bill, giving him a big tip because I just don't care. Paige is thinking about something else when she asks to see the Target Box, and that's all right, because I'm thinking about other things too. Companionship. "Okay, Paige, let's go see the Target Box."

JETS OVERHEAD

I am not an alcoholic, which for some reason I feel is important to make clear. Of course, anyone who declares "I'm not an alcoholic" is pretty suspect. No one has stood up at an AA meeting and said, "I am an alcoholic" without first going through a period of declaring the exact opposite. The simple fact is that I am stone-dry sober 362 days a year, and don't even think about alcohol. I don't drink egg nog on Christmas, champagne on New Year's Eve, and I am completely oblivious to the aisles of alcohol at the grocery store. I keep a little cheap wine in the house for cooking, but that's it. For me, drinking has always been a social thing. If my friends are going out for drinks, so am I. So perhaps I'm sober all year because I have no one to drink with. But there are three days each year when I head to Chicago and go on a bender, and the first thing I do is try and find someone who will drink with me.

I never thought one way or another about alcohol when I was younger. My first beer was in sixth grade, much earlier than anyone else I knew, and I distinctly remember it. I was staying with a friend at his parent's cottage on Lake Michigan and they let us camp out one night on our own. We had a small fire going on the beach while a little farther down some older kids, probably high school age, had built a large bon-fire and were gathered round as someone strummed a guitar. We didn't dare go down and join them, but one of the boys, long-haired and shirtless, had wandered down toward us, twisting his feet into the sand as he walked.

"What are you guys doing?" he asked.

"Nothing," my friend said, sitting on a log by our tent, not looking up as he drew lines in the sand with his hiking stick.

"We're camping," I defended.

"Camping?" the boy asked, "And doing what else, earning your Boy Scout badges?"

"No."

"Telling ghost stories?"

"No."

"Making s'mores?"

"No."

"Good. Those things are gay, gay and gay. But so is camping. Who the hell wants to sleep outside with the bugs and bad weather, just for the hell of it?"

"We get to stay up as late as we want," my friend said.

"Whoa. Now that's crazy."

"We get to do whatever we want," I added.

"And what do you want to do?"

Neither of us responded.

"Hold on." We waited as the boy wandered off, returning a few minutes later with a six pack of beer, the cans dangling from their plastic rings. He pulled off a can and threw it right at me, hard, so I'd either have to catch it or duck. I caught it, as did my friend, and we watched the boy peel a can off for himself, crack the top and hold up his beer, shouting "Cheers!" I didn't pause, didn't really think about it, and just mimicked the boy, opening my beer and echoing, "Cheers!" My friend watched cautiously as the boy took a long chug and I took a mouthful, swirling it in my mouth and finally swallowing. My first beer, and though I didn't feel guilty, I thought it tasted like swamp water.

I liked doing what others were doing, I liked being part of the group, suddenly feeling a connection to the older kids farther down, whom I could hear singing the chorus to a Kiss rock ballad. I felt cool and I liked it.

"Fuck yeah," the boy shouted, "making s'mores and drinking Coors. That's fuckin' camping."

I wonder what I would have said no to. Had he passed me a cigarette, I'm sure I would have smoked it. Probably a joint, too. Were he dropping acid, munching shrooms or breaking out lines of coke, I'm not sure where I would have drawn the line. I've always been pretty stupid about trying something new. Not stupid in the way one miscalculates the pros and cons and comes to the wrong conclusion, but stupid in the way one doesn't even think about it. If someone else is doing it, I'm in. I just need the invite. With that attitude, I was lucky to make it as far as I had.

I had two beers that night and wouldn't drink again until high school, but I was finally aware of alcohol. My parents didn't drink, didn't talk about it, and all the billboards and commercials pitching beer might as well have been marketing fertilizer or shoe polish, for all they noticed. I knew beer existed but didn't understand why. Now I knew it was a lifestyle. It was a magic trick for taking the mundane, camping out, playing ping-pong in someone's basement, or hanging out in the woods by the railroad track, and making it cool.

Yet I managed to stay in control. I didn't play any sports in college, but took up running, and seemed to have fallen into a pretty good group. We went to bars and apartment parties most weekends, but drinking was secondary. There were a few binge weekends, after a big football win like Illinois' upset of Iowa, blowing off steam after finals, and of course anyone's twenty-first birthday. But we drank in moderation, unlike the other kids chugging their Irish car bombs, ordering round after round of shots and doing keg stands. I saw the stumbling drunks late at night, smelled the puke on the streets Sunday morning, and knew there was a whole other level of drinking, but I didn't want any part of it because my friends weren't doing it. I hadn't been invited. It wasn't until after college, getting an apartment just south of Wrigley Field, that I would get that invitation.

My buddy Schatz, who also just graduated from Illinois, got a job at some mergers and acquisitions firm, and we found an apartment with two of his friends from business school. They had four friends who took the apartment above, most of them traders, and our units had a rickety back balcony connected by stairs. As I met everyone I learned the first rule, which was a clear indicator of how we were going to live. The first rule was that there would always be an open keg. Whichever unit bought it could keep it on their floor. The moment it went dry, it was up to the other unit to replace it. We called her Old Betsy.

Our unit was usually the slower one to replace the keg, but by slower I just mean it might take a day or two. McCarran, who lived upstairs and was the ringleader of our exploits, didn't appreciate our tardiness and showed up with a chess clock to go alongside Old Betsy, with our apartment number written on each side. Whenever the keg went dry, she showed up on the other unit's back door with the clock running. If that wasn't clear enough, McCarran usually followed it up by shouting through the back door, "You're on the clock, motherfuckers!" He always talked proudly of the time he woke us, at 4:30 AM on a Tuesday morning, to declare he just finished the keg.

"You've got problems!" I shouted from my slumber in a back bedroom, looking at the clock and wondering if any beer stores were open and if I could make it there and back before heading to work.

We lived like that for four years before the situation began showing signs of wear. Quaid was the first to move out, taking a job in D.C., but The Dawg took his place without much trouble. P-Train got a girlfriend, and though we all had girlfriends here and there, she was the first one to change the dynamic and start pointing out how we were in our mid-twenties and living like frat boys. I don't even remember her real name because we called her Yoko. I think it was Anne or Jan. Maybe Janet. Regardless, she did have a point and some of us sensed it was time to move on. I had a girlfriend, a serious girlfriend and spent most nights at her place, while others like McCarran felt the only solution to keep things going was to turn the partying up a notch. Once a month, I fielded the obligatory call to go out with the old crew.

"Tail!" McCarran shouted, staring across the street at two girls hailing a cab, far enough away that I had no idea what they looked like. It was McCarran, Schatz and me, sitting outside a bar on a Saturday night.

"When did you start drinking?" I asked, on my second beer and knowing there's no way I'll catch up to McCarran, who's slightly slurring, can't keep quiet for thirty seconds and is referring to himself in the third person. He's wasted yet holding it together, which is pretty standard for McCarran.

"Fourth grade. At my cousin's wedding. Southside wedding all the way."

"This binge. When did you start this binge?"

"Clean your ears, I just told you. Fourth grade. Straight through 'til now."

"Fair enough. Today," I said, "when did you start drinking today?"

"He started yesterday," Schatz said. "He left the pit early."

"They let you do that?" I asked.

"Who's going to stop me?" McCarran said. "When you make that much money in one day, you can go whenever the fuck you want."

I remembered seeing a headline in the paper about the DOW being up, but didn't read it. It didn't mean anything to me, but things like the DOW and NASDAQ futures were the lifeblood of most of my roommates. "So you quit early?"

"McCarran doesn't quit," McCarran said. "I left early. I left smart. Markets were up crazy most of the day and the Daddy Mac, the Chi-Town Hustler, was in big. I made all I could and people were getting stupid. Today's the day that options expire. Some people were trying to keep the rally going while others were trying to minimize their losses. A lot of dumb money was flowing in both directions, and I know enough to stay clear of that. Went to the club and worked out, grabbed some sushi and have been hitting it ever since."

"You were up all night?"

"Home by 1:00 last night, but up until 4:00. Surprised you didn't hear me below. That biddy left at eight this morning, when I decided it was time for another beer."

"So how many beers do you think you've had today?"

"What's it now, almost 8:00? That's twelve hours, figure two beers an hour, at least. So that's a case."

"Jesus," Schatz said.

"Jesus what?"

"That's a lot of drinking."

"That's a lot of pissing," he said. "And don't give me that shit. You've done your share of benders. Just 'cause you don't keep track doesn't mean you haven't put away a case before."

"He's gotcha there," I said. "Remember Michigan. Old Town last year.

St. Pat's. Ugly Fest."

"You're not any better," McCarran said to me.

"So we're all a bunch of alcoholics?"

"We're not alcoholics. An alcoholic is someone who can't stop drinking when it's no longer fun."

"That's the definition?" I asked. We never thought about being alcoholics, really. There were only two things we knew about alcohol. First, drinking could make anything fun. Drinking was fun. Second, drinking more was more fun. There were no limits to this wisdom, no exceptions, caveats, or considerations beyond those two points.

"Oh, I'm sure you and your psycho-babble friends have another definition, but that's what I go by."

"There are plenty of alcoholics who think they're having fun."

"Not just for the drinker. For everyone around them. When it's no longer fun for everyone involved, and they still can't stop, that's your sign. My problem is I'm always having fun and so is everyone around me, so I can't ever be an alcoholic."

"That's your problem?" Schatz asked. "Really?"

"That's a mighty convenient definition," I added.

"And don't worry about yourself," McCarran said, looking at me. "Just because you put away a case on the weekend doesn't mean you're an alcoholic. You drink that much because we do. You're lucky too. You know how many of those money-signers in the pit are cokeheads?"

"What does that have to do with me?"

"'Cause if I were a cokehead like them, you'd be one too."

"Perhaps," I nodded, worried that my restraint was tethered to McCarran's restraint.

"Probably," Schatz said.

"Definitely," McCarran finished.

I sipped my beer, swirled it in my mouth and wondered. I'm the psychiatrist, but sometimes I felt like McCarran had better insights into people, even after drinking a case of beer. Or especially after a case of beer.

"Money-signers?" Schatz asked, a step behind as usual.

"Traders," McCarran said, "moving their hands to make trades, like sign language." He started flipping his hands around, making buy and sell gestures that neither of us understood, finishing up by giving Schatz and me the double bird. "It's like we're doing sign-language, but you know what each sign means?"

"What?" Schatz asked.

"Money. Every time I make a sign, every time I make a trade, it means money. Every fucking time. It's like the close-captioned access channel for printing money."

"If you became a cokehead, that doesn't mean I'd be one too," I argued.

"I make my own decisions."

"Bullshit!" McCarran stated. "You would join me in a second, at least before Margaret was in the picture. And it's not because I'd force you or any sort of peer pressure crap; it's because you don't give a shit."

"No way," I said.

"What'd you do today?"

"What?"

"What…" McCarran started, throwing out more signs with each word, slow-talking his words with the lisp of a deaf person, "…did you do… today?"

"I went to the Art Museum."

"With?"

"With Margaret."

"You went to the Art Museum with your girlfriend rather than spending the day with me, celebrating what a great trader I am. And did you enjoy it?"

"Yeah."

"Like I said. You'll go along with anything. You're just glad to be doing something."

"Bite me."

"Bite me? That's all you got? Bite –," McCarran stopped and stared with wide eyes behind Schatz, to where the bouncer was checking IDs. "Twelve o'clock. Tail supreme. But don't look, Schatz."

"Where?" Schatz asked.

"Don't look," McCarran repeated. "Just wait. She's looking this way. Play it cool and I'll tell you when it's safe. Just hold on."

I glanced behind Schatz and earnestly said, "Wow. Just wow."

"Just your type," McCarran said.

Schatz was gripping both arms of his chair, looking every which way but behind, like a puppy just learning to hold it. "Is she blonde or brunette?"

"With a body like that," McCarran said, "does it matter? All right, you can look now, but play it cool."

And no matter how drunk McCarran was, and no matter how many times he'd done it before, he'd always been able to make Schatz believe the most beautiful girl in the city was right behind him. Schatz turned around to see the girl having her ID checked, who's barely five foot and easily pushing two hundred pounds, readjusting her sparkly red top and mini-skirt.

"Fuck you," Schatz said.

McCarran roared. It never got old, watching Schatz turn back in embarrassment, lifting his beer and taking a long swig. I couldn't stop laughing either. This had been my life the past few years, lots of booze, childish jokes, and lots of laughter. This had been my life, and I'd been fine with it, but things were about to change. "So I'm thinking of popping the

32

question," I said.

"What?" Schatz asked. "You're going to propose? To Margaret?"

"No, to Pink Lemonade Girl," McCarran said, referring to some girl I briefly dated, who we now referenced with the name of some punchline to a joke nobody remembered; we just laughed when it was repeated. "Of course, Margaret."

"That's a big step buddy. You really think you're ready?"

"Yeah, I do."

"Well congratu-fucking-lations!" McCarran shouted, and I could tell he was sincere and it actually felt good. McCarran's the type who I wouldn't trust watching a goldfish for a few days, but was the first one to show up at the wake when my mom passed and got me in touch with a company that does estate sales, even checked them out with the Better Business Bureau. With McCarran, there were a handful of things that were important, and for those things he pulled through, all the way. But with McCarran, everything else was a huge fucking joke. If I had a million dollars, McCarran was the one I'd most trust to watch over it, but he's the one I'd least trust with the last slice of Lou Malnatti's. "She's a good girl. A really good girl. You two will make a good couple."

"Thanks." I didn't think I'd need affirmation, but was surprisingly glad to get it.

"So let's see, I predict you'll be living in the suburbs with a kid in two years. Maybe north shore but probably out west, like St. Charles or Glen Ellen. Actually, you're from Lemont, right? That's where you'll end up, I have no doubt."

"Now I'm having second thoughts."

"Like a turtle returning eggs, you'll be back in Lemont in no time."

"There's no way I'm going back to Lemont."

"You've swum in the big sea, little turtle, now it's time to go home."

"No way."

"Where's Margaret from anyway?"

"Colorado."

"That's right. A bit of a hippie chick. I bet it'll be a bit of a hippie-dippie wedding too."

"That means drunk hippie bridesmaids," Schatz added.

"Nice," McCarran said, giving Schatz a fist-bump. "Drunk hippie bridesmaids who are from out of town. Fish in a barrel, and no need to call anyone back."

"Margaret's going to warn all her girlfriends about you."

"She better. Then I'm Bad Boy McCarran. Who doesn't want to be with the bad boy for a night?"

"Shit. There's no stopping you, is there?"

"Absolutely no fucking way. Does Margaret have a sister?"

"Thankfully, no."

"How about a brother? For Schatz?"

"Fuck you."

"No brother, either," I said. "Just like me, an only child whose parents have passed."

"Sorry to hear that," Schatz said.

"It wasn't yesterday, but a few years ago. Before we met."

"Still sorry." Schatz and McCarran both attended my mother's funeral, a somber event in the midst of a life of partying, and they both got awkward when it came up.

"Fewer toasts," I said.

"Fewer toasts," McCarran agreed, but wanted to change the subject. "How'd you two meet, anyway?"

"At a class."

"A class?"

"A writing class," Schatz clarified.

"You write?"

"He wrote a book."

I rolled my eyes, knowing this was the type of thing I'd be made fun of for the next year or two, the type of thing I would have happily made fun of someone else for two years. "Yeah, it's nothing."

"So where do I get this book? What's it about?"

"It's a mystery, sort of. But you're not going to read it unless you steal my laptop."

"What's it called?"

"*The Gothic Century.*"

"Have you read it?" McCarran asked Schatz.

"Yes. It's good."

"Well damn. I'm going to have to read this thing. So you're taking writing classes on the side and picking up future wives. Is Margaret a writer too?"

"A bit. She does short stories, some journaling."

"Of course she does. She's a photographer, right?"

"Yep, portraiture."

"Portraiture? You're definitely marrying a hippy chick. A cool chick, but a hippie nonetheless. That's a good thing though, because with what you make talking to people about their problems, and with what she makes asking them to say cheese, you're going to be living in the poor house."

"I think we'll be all right."

"All right? Really? Is that all we're shooting for?" McCarran asked.

I smiled, opened my mouth to respond, but was interrupted by the loud swoosh from a pack of fighter jets flying overhead. It was the weekend of the Air and Water Show and the whole city went quiet as the extraordinary machines circled overhead. It's Saturday, when spectators lined the lake front and made a day of it, while we tried not to look up unless we were certain one was overhead, maintaining a been-there seen-that attitude. It was all right to watch on Friday, when they practiced for the show, like we had a backstage pass, but Saturday was for the common people, and joining them would have made us common. We couldn't have that. Instead, we all drank our beers without acknowledging the jets screeching overhead or the hallowed bellow of their afterburn.

MUST SLEEP

Must sleep. That's what I'm thinking, but of course, thinking about sleep only makes it that much more difficult.

I'm amazed how well everything is going. I showed Paige the Target Box, let her brush her hand along the soft wood and leather straps, press against the polished brass rivets, and study the lock. "This is why you're going to Chicago?"

"Partially," I say. "It's a reason to go, but I also want to see the city again and have some fun."

Paige smiles, a sweet seductive smile and moves toward me, her left finger running along the dresser where the Target Box sits. She reaches for my side, and I place a hand behind her shoulder, my thumb just resting on the back of her neck. But then I interrupt the moment by throwing a word between us.

"Actually," I say, letting the word hang for a moment so she knows I'm about to pivot, but without knowing where. "I was thinking," I continue, gauging her expression as I ask, "How would you like to come with me?"

"To Chicago?"

"Yes. It'd be fun. An impromptu getaway."

"A whole weekend in Chicago? Just the two of us?"

"Yep. With nothing to do but have fun."

"I don't know."

"When was the last time you did something spontaneous?"

Paige looks around the room, at her hand on my side, which she lowers. "About five minutes ago, when I came up here."

"Good point."

"But before that? It's been years. I don't do spontaneous."

"Now's your chance."

Paige looks around again, and inquisitively stares at the Target Box. "You promise you're not doing anything illegal?"

"I promise."

"A promise. I guess that's all I've got to go on."

"Cross my heart," I say, keeping the next line to myself.

"A second grade promise."

"I promise we'll have fun."

36

"How about this?" Paige says. "I've had plenty to drink. How about I say maybe, and then you ask me again in the morning?"

"I'll take a maybe."

"Then you've got a maybe."

"But," I say.

"But what?"

"But I think," I say, pausing because I don't really want to say it, "I think we should take it slow. Slower, at least."

"Slow?"

I glance at the bed and my gaze reluctantly returns to Paige. "I'd like to be a gentleman," I lie. The bottom line is sex can be viewed as one of the most important interactions between two people, or it can be a casual tryst that means nothing at all. I'm not sure which of those extremes scares me the most, but I'm not ready for either. Not now, not to start the weekend.

Paige exhales, "Grrrr."

"Was that a growl?" I ask.

"No," Paige quickly answers. "Er, yes. I'm possibly going to spend a weekend with you, and yet I'm somehow disappointed to find out you're a gentleman."

"Not as disappointed as I am."

Paige nibbles on her lower lip and takes a big breath. "I wouldn't bet on it."

And for ten seconds I stare at her and am so ready to throw out being a gentleman, so ready to nibble on those lips myself and just ravish her, the weekend be damned. Twenty seconds pass. Thirty seconds of temptation. I finally exhale and mutter, "We should get some sleep."

And that's how I'm lying here, on my side, with Paige next to me in one of my t-shirts.

Must sleep.

I've turned away from her, but her hand is resting on my thigh, and the side of her foot rests lightly on my calf. Her breath and her heat fill the room, and her presence is the only thought in my mind.

Must sleep.

She probably didn't think I meant it, that once we got into bed I'd make a move. If she were having second thoughts, she would have complained at some point, said we needed another room, one with double beds, or informed me that I should be sleeping on the couch. Something. But her willingness to wash her face, change into an oversized t-shirt with I-don't-know-what underneath and then crawl into bed next to me, only confirms that I could roll over, make my move and she wouldn't say no.

Must sleep.

It's not that I'm not horny. Hell no, and especially not right now. Just because I haven't been with anyone for what is fast approaching eternity doesn't mean I've lost those primal instincts. But I don't like them. I don't like seeing some bikini-clad model on TV or a magazine cover, and suddenly having those sexual thoughts rise up and start replaying in my head, taking control. Most of the time I can still push them back down, ignore them until they're no longer part of my life. Work helps. Running helps. Mowing the lawn. Doing something, anything that keeps the gears moving and the thoughts on moving forward, step by step. But there is still downtime, still inescapable moments.

I used to have a few porno mags, picked up at a gas station while making the drive to Georgia, but they don't belong in my house and I quickly threw them out. My house is a temple. Pornography would only desecrate it. As for my body, it's far from a temple. It's a giant tangle of suppressed thoughts, hopes that will never come to pass and fears that have already been marked with a time and date, and somewhere in that tangle is that ancient urge to fuck. Just fuck and fuck and fuck and eventually pass out spent and thoughtless. And to be thoughtless, that might be better than the fucking.

Must sleep.

I couldn't have had this control when I was twenty-two. And it's not just because my sex drive was stronger, although it probably was. Back then, it seemed perfectly natural to think about girls, girls, girls. Everyone I knew did the same, and the girls were thinking about us boys, so where was the harm?

I think that's what has changed. I've realized how what seemed like such a simple and pure instinct, is so tightly coupled with the unbearable awkwardness of relationships. I know how even a simple kiss can change everything between two people. What does it mean? Do you like her? Does she like you? Do you like her more or less than she likes you? Are you going to call? Will you hold hands in public? Are you boyfriend and girlfriend? Awkwardness at every step.

The worst part is, when we get older, we think we can avoid it. We think those questions are juvenile, that we've outgrown the anticipation and excitement, that whatever happens, happens. And yes, we are able to suppress our feelings better. We become hardened to the pain inflicted by others, the pain we inflict on them. We sweep our pain aside and say that's life and act like we've come to terms with this state of relationships, equipped with a resolve called maturity. It may be life, but it still hurts.

Must sleep.

And I did try the way without feelings. Once. I found her on the internet, an escort from Atlanta. Six hundred dollars for two hours, although I didn't know what we would do for two full hours. She knocked on the door, and just like the ad said, told me her name was Skye. "Is it really?" I asked. She smiled and said she got that all the time, but yes, it really was. This bothered me immensely, starting off with a lie.

In retrospect, I was all right with the first lie, that she was more interested in me than the six hundred dollars, but I wanted to know her real name. We talked a little longer, small talk, but I couldn't help coming back around and asking again, "Really, what's your real name?"

Skye persisted, but I was not having sex with someone whose name I didn't even know, so we talked some more. She sat next to me on the couch, running her hand through my hair and massaging my neck. I kept thinking about the same thing she was, the seven hundred dollars in my pocket. I didn't care about the money, not even the extra hundred as a tip. I cared that she cared about it. That she was able to get past all those emotions that come packaged with what we were about to do. That I couldn't tell which of her words were real and which were artificial. I'm a psychologist, I listen to people talk all day, so I should know this. But she probably couldn't discern the two either. We talked more; I made her laugh. I asked about her past, which she seemed surprisingly open about.

And once we were comfortable with each other, once we were in a place that, were it anyone else in any other situation, I would have thought us to be friends, I asked for what I really wanted.

"In all seriousness," I said, "is your name really Skye?"

"It's Beth," she confessed. "Plain old Beth."

I lied and told her it wasn't a plain name. It was a plain name, but it was also a real name, and that was so much more important.

We talked some more, and not surprisingly my instincts as a psychologist came out, asking how she felt about her past, how her relationships affected her and lo and behold, we had a breakthrough. (I don't even believe in "breakthroughs." It's not that they don't occasionally happen, but patients too often aim for them, expect them, and that's usually not the way it works.) So for seven hundred dollars, I paid Beth to cry on my shoulder and tell me about how her father treated her like shit, how her boyfriend got her pregnant and hit her in the stomach, told her beforehand he was going to do it, and then took her to the hospital. Once the doctors started asking questions, how he walked out the door, packed his things, and was never seen again. How once doctors got her to confess he had hit her, she said it was during a fight. She guessed they knew that she had allowed it, and they probably thought the baby was better off than being raised by a crazy mother who allowed her boyfriend to lay her down in the backseat of their car, parked four blocks from the hospital, a mother who closed her eyes and clenched her fists into tight balls because there was nothing to hold on to, the mother who didn't flinch when her boyfriend said, "I'm sorry" before dealing the blow that would cause the abortion.

And somehow we try to pretend that sex isn't complicated.

Must sleep.

Skye got her seven hundred dollars, Beth got a little closure, and I got a neck massage and another restless night.

Must sleep.

Which is why I'm lying here, watching the electric alarm clock while all I can feel is Paige's body heat seething around me. The room is silent, and I can sense her waiting, wondering what the hell I'm doing. What sort of guy picks her up in a bar, invites her to Chicago for the weekend, and doesn't even try to put a move on her while they're lying in bed together.

Must sleep.

Paige is drunk, there's no doubt about that. I only had a few drinks, but it's been so long that my tolerance is nothing. I'm just hoping the buzz helps me fall asleep quickly, helps me stop thinking about how easy it would be to roll over and grab Paige by the small of her back, pull her head into me, and start with an impassioned kiss. And then I feel movement, a hand sliding against the sheets, Paige placing her hand on my hip, the highpoint of my imprint tucked beneath the covers. She gives an ever so slight pull and I think must sleep, must sleep, must sleep….

I roll around a little, acting as if I'd already been sound asleep and something just disturbed me, finally settling into my previous turned-away position, reciting my mantra, must sleep, must sleep, must sleep…

Finally Paige pulls her hand away and I so badly want to follow it, turning like a marionette, pulled by one taught string. Must sleep, must sleep…

Paige sighs and then rolls away, so we're back-to-back like a married couple going to sleep mad at each other. Must sleep…

And I count the seconds and repeat my mantra, must sleep, must sleep, must sleep, over and over and over, and must sleep, must sleep, must sleep, over and over and over, and must sleep, must sleep, must sleep, over and over and over…

And then it's morning.

CRACKER BARREL PRIDE

When I wake, Paige is already up. I can hear her using her cell phone to call work. "I need to take a personal day," she says and that's it. No fake cough or sore throat, no attempt at explaining what she probably doesn't want to explain to her boss. Just the facts, and I admire that.

I hear the faucet running for a while and know she has nothing to work with, no brush or makeup or whatever else she needs, but when the door opens she looks good. She still looks like she just woke up, still the morning after a night of drinking and sleeping in a hotel bed with a stranger, but she looks comfortable with that. Paige has pulled everything together and there's a sparkle in her eye, a little bit of mirth beneath her tired eyes, and it looks good. Since we didn't have sex, our interaction isn't too awkward, but we shared a room together, a bed, and at the end of the day we are still strangers about to take part in a journey together. It certainly could have been awkward, but Paige says, "Good morning" like it was the thousandth time she's said it to me and she would say it a thousand more times.

"Good morning," I reply, sitting up. I stare at her eyes, nothing else, and tell her, "I think it's going to be a good day today."

Paige smiles.

"I think we're going to have fun on our little adventure."

"Good. That's what I want to hear."

I grab my bag and head into the bathroom, saying, "Give me thirty" as I check my watch. I emerge twenty-six minutes later, showered, shaven and dressed, with my packed bag around my shoulder. I pick up the Target Box and carefully hold it against my side. "Ready?"

We exit the room and head down toward the elevators. "I remember asking lots of questions about that thing, but I don't remember you giving me any answers."

"Then you remember everything. Now, I assume you want to stop by home first? I figure we can eat on the road?"

Paige lives about twenty minutes outside of Carbondale, in the middle unit of a line of townhouses that circle a small pond. She doesn't have me park down the street or anything like that, but when we pull into the driveway she sits for a moment, staring at her house. If there ever were a time to back out, a time to say this is crazy, now is that time. And letting a

41

strange man into her house might be a good time to say this is crazy.

"I can wait in the car," I say.

"Are you sure, it might be a bit?"

"Is there a place I can get a coffee?"

"There's a Dunkin Donuts if you go back the way we came, just take Park to Rendleman."

"Okay, how long do I have?"

"Give me an hour."

"I'll be back in an hour. Do you want anything?"

"No, I'm good for now."

I watch Paige get out and enter her front door without looking back. What is she thinking? Identical homes, tied together, painted an innocuous tan, an attempt for identical structure to house residents who surely have nothing in common. I imagine an elderly couple, living out their last years. A large family whose parents work many hours near minimum wage. A lone man in his late thirties, who moved in as a layover onto bigger things, yet hasn't left and probably never will. And of course Paige, a fun-loving, risk-taking woman who has agreed to spend a weekend with me, someone she met just over twelve hours ago. Paige is attractive, I can come out and say it, I need to say it to myself, but she's also looking for something; she's curious enough, or hopeful enough, that she's willing to take a gamble and spend the weekend with someone she just met.

This shouldn't be that outrageous, considering people meet at bars and have sex all the time. They go back to a stranger's houses in the middle of the night and do what should be the most intimate thing a couple can do. And yet, going on a weekend trip, spending time together, some of it sober, and actually being stuck with that person, that seems like the bigger risk. I don't know why. I look along the row of townhomes and think, Paige is the only resident going on an adventure today. Good for Paige, I think without any sarcasm.

I spend that hour looking for a Starbucks. When it's not just to wake me up, when I have an hour to sip and enjoy my coffee, then I like it bitter and black. I stop and ask at two different gas stations, where the second says if there is a Starbucks, it'd be down on the SIU campus. I drive around for a half hour, ask a gaggle of college kids who are on campus early, for band camp or RA meetings or whatever, but they don't think there is one. They recommend some local coffee house where students go to study, but I decide to drive around some more and eventually return to Paige's empty handed.

She's ready, on the dot, and we put her suitcase in the trunk and she gets in. I give her a look, slightly serious, to see if she's changed her mind.

"What?" she asks.

"Nothing. You ready for this?"

"Is there any reason I shouldn't be?"

"No, just making sure."

"Oh, I'm ready. The question is if you're ready?"

"Am I ready?" I pause. "If I may quote my much younger self, fuck yeah I'm ready."

"Fuck yeah," Paige repeats, and we're off. Paige guides me to Illinois 13 which leads to I-57 which, in about five hours, should get us to Chicago. I'm tempted to quote the Blues Brothers, but think better of it.

I'm still craving coffee, we're both hungry and with an hour of driving behind us we decide to stop at a roadside Cracker Barrel for a late breakfast. I like how the Cracker Barrel is built to look like a wooden lodge you happen to discover while backpacking through unfamiliar woods, yet is really a chain restaurant found at every fourth exit. We walk through the folksy store in front, its shelves filled with small town stereotypes: Norman Rockwell prints, ceramic figurines, caramel apples and jars of marmalade. I can accept all of these because of another small town stereotype: the ability to make one hell of a breakfast. I'm willing to look past these tropes as long as I get my big breakfast and coffee.

Senior citizens occupy the tables and booths here, the only people who can afford a leisurely breakfast on a Friday morning. Even though I have all day, I can't help feeling the pace is too slow. Our waitress, Jennie, can't be much over eighteen, and likes to chat up her other tables, hand on hip, giving us no more than a raised eyebrow to let us know she'll be with us when she's ready. She's got a scar above her lip and I notice she talks to us with a little less twang then she had at the table next to us. I've turned my coffee cup over, cupping it in both hands, and nod as soon as she says coffee, sending her off while we peruse the menu.

"What are you having?" I ask.

She reaches over, flips my menu closed and taps the back of the menu, pointing to the Fruit 'n Yogurt parfait, at which I look at her like she's crazy. "I like to eat healthy," she informs me.

"That's nice and all, but I believe you're forgetting where you are."

She looks around. "A Cracker Barrel?"

"No."

"I'm not at a Cracker Barrel?"

"Yes Paige, you are at a Cracker Barrel, but you are also on vacation. Which means you can get something like what I'm getting. Listen to this," I say, reading from the menu, "Uncle Hershel's Favorite, which is two eggs cooked to order, grits, sawmill gravy over buttermilk biscuits, hash brown casserole and hickory-smoked country ham. I couldn't make that up if I tried."

"That doesn't even sound good."

"Speak for yourself. But don't tell me your craving soggy fruit drenched in yogurt. Not when you're on vacation and can have anything you want."

She goes through the menu again while I look around. The old men are looking at her, and I realize I'm with the best-looking girl in the place, the one that everyone else sneaks a look at from behind their menus or with swiveled heads, pretending to look for the waitress. Of course it's not a fair contest, as Paige has twenty to thirty years on most of the women in here. Regardless, it feels good to be with a beautiful woman, and it also feels good to be with the best looking one in the room, no matter what the competition. Pride, one of the seven deadly sins. Back home, I've lost almost all sense of pride, so a little bit's good for me. It feels a little normal.

"I love bacon," my blue-ribbon companion informs me, ordering a side when Jennie comes back around. And near the end, while I'm still eating and she's finished with her bacon as well as her assortment of strawberries, blueberries and raspberries soaked in yogurt, Paige orders another side of bacon.

"That's the spirit," I tell her.

"As long as we're on vacation," she replies.

She understands. We're out to have fun.

On the way out, we stop on the front porch of this purposely rustic building where a row of rocking chairs rest idly. With coffees in hand I sit in one and Paige takes the chair next to me. Without a word, we rock and sip, back and forth, enjoying a moment of just being, something that's much easier to do in the morning, with the sun coming out and a wide open day opening before us. "Sure is a mighty purty day," I say, watching the few clouds in the sky before they burn off in the afternoon heat.

Paige looks at me funny and asks, "What?"

I continue, drawing out my vowels and adding a country twang, "I say-ed, it shore is lookin' to be a might purty day. Pur-ty indeed."

"Okay."

"Just doing my best country-bumpkin impression. Not very good, I guess."

"It's fine," Paige says. "Cliché, but fine."

"I guess cliché is what I was aiming for."

Paige and I rock for a bit, watching the cars on the highway, with empty fields on both sides. "You know," Paige finally says, "that cliché is my grandparents. They lived out in Exeter, had their own farm. They'd sit out on the front porch most summer nights, just rocking away, not doing much of anything. Opa liked to drink a few beers, Oma smoked her Virginia Slims, and they'd just sit out there and rock 'til the sun went down."

"Were they watching anything?"

"Oh no. They were deep country. If a single car went by, that'd make their conversation for the night. Who it was, where they were going. But most nights there was nothing."

"What did you do?"

"I used to stay with them a few weeks in the summer, and when I was younger I'd go sit on the stairs or play in the yard, but once I got older, around the teenage years, I couldn't take it. I'd go out and read for a bit, but I was dying to go inside and watch TV, listen to the radio, or call a friend. They didn't need conversation. In fact, they didn't want any conversation. They enjoyed just sitting and enjoy their vices. I remember complaining to my mom that I couldn't go back, not for a whole two weeks, as it was so boring. When I finally started getting summer jobs, it became a great excuse not to stay with them."

"I have to admit," I say, "I kind of understand it now, the pleasure of just sitting, doing nothing."

"Doing nothing and having nothing to do. I totally get it. Hell, that's kind of a goal of mine, to be able to sit and do nothing and be happy with it. I do my yoga, and I've tried mediation, but my mind needs to do something."

"I know. Maybe someday we'll be able to sit and do nothing, but not yet."

"It's a shame," Paige says, "how much I hated visiting them near the end. I probably didn't even hide it, my contempt for their country lifestyle."

"You were a kid. That's what kids do."

"I know, just a shame. I think I'd like spending an evening with Oma and Opa."

"That's nice," I say, and we impersonate them for a while, spending our time on the porch, not doing or saying anything, just appreciating. I realize I want to get something, and tell Paige I'll be right back as I head inside and return with a plastic bag in my hand.

We walk to the car, and for the first time I don't go to her side of the car and open the door. I do make her wait while I get in first, but as soon as I unlock her side, she slides in and sees the envelope resting on the dash, her name printed across the front.

Paige looks at it carefully while I back out of our spot, ignoring her as she reaches for the envelope and opens it. The card has a simple sketch of a small bunny rabbit standing in a patch of daisies, a half-eaten carrot at its feet. The inside was blank, unsure of what this bunny wants to convey, so I have carefully printed the words "Thank You" inside.

"What's this for?"

"I just wanted to thank you for going on this trip with me," I say nonchalantly. "I think we're going to have fun."

She leans over, stretches across my hand on the stick shift, and gives me a kiss on the cheek. "That's so nice…"

"I hope I'm going north?" I interrupt as we get on the highway.

I drive for a little while, and I seem to have put Paige in a really good mood. We're not talking much, but she seems happy to just sit and listen to the radio, watching the outside pass while the air conditioner keeps us comfortable. I know it's the card that has made her happy, and though that's what I wanted, it seems too much. So after pulling her close, I push.

"So how come you didn't try out for cheerleading your senior year?"

Paige turns her head and puzzles a bit, wondering why I'm asking this now. "I don't want to talk about it," she says. That seems to have put her good mood in check. She wants to change the subject and asks, "So when are you going to tell me what's in the Target Box?"

"Yeah, I don't really want to talk about that either."

For Paige, it's tit-for-tat. I ask a hard question, she asks a hard question. I think that's healthier than my push-pull, but of course we'd both be better off with a live and let live approach. It's amazing how deep these little things run. Life strategies. Tit-for-tat. Push-pull. Live and let live. Obla-di Obla-da, life does go on.

Anyway, I pushed with my last question, so I can give a little here. "Just so you know, I'm going to bury it."

"Bury it?"

"Exactly."

"Bury it where?"

"I'm not quite sure yet. I'll figure it out when we get there."

"Do you need me to be part of this?"

"Not at all. It's my tradition. My reason. I'll take care of it. I'll just go out for an hour, maybe a little more, come back, and that's that. That's about the only thing I do know."

"I hope you also know how weird this is."

"I know that too. And I apologize. Just some old tradition I need to keep going."

I can see Paige thinking, but the depth of her next question astonishes me.

"I can only think of two things you put in the ground. Living things, like trees and flowers, or dead things. Now I assume there's nothing alive in that box…"

"There's nothing dead in it either," I assure her.

"I didn't think there was. But burying that box, for whatever mysterious reason you do it, which one is it like? Is it more like planting something alive to grow, or is it like burying something dead, to decay and disappear?"

"That's a good question," I admit. "That's a really good question."

RETURN

Most of Illinois is farmland. We've been driving for hours, passing tiny clusters of people separated by tract after tract of open farmland, crisscrossed by country roads. But as we approach Chicago it starts changing, and the changes come quickly. First there is the sprawl land, the area where housing prices are considered cheap, as long as you don't mind living that far from the city. There is the constant building of subdivisions, strip malls, schools, parks, and small businesses. There are still open areas out here, state parks and barren fields that for some reason or another have been skipped over by the developers, sure to be recaptured in time.

Supposedly there is a housing boom. Cheap houses being chased by cheaper mortgages to be flipped, resold and repeated. When a small consumer product is the must-have item, like Motorola's Razr cell phone was last year, then billions get spent, quarterly profits blow past expectations and companies become titans of industry. I can only imagine how much money is being passed when the must-have item isn't a new phone but a new house. I have no idea where the money is coming from, but it's my understanding that everyone's a winner. Looking at the new homes, imagining the swing sets going up and new families moving in, hosting barbecues and birthday parties, I have a moment of naïve hope that is quickly crushed, not by knowledge of how construction works or mortgages or anything financial, but how life works. These sprawls of construction dot the highway like spores expanding from their skyscrapered host, transitioning into the true suburbia, a patchwork of long established towns, pressed against each other, one after another.

To a certain degree each town is different, depending on what fleck of commonality it grew out of. Some house the rich and affluent city people who need towering mansions with manicured yards. Some are more comfortable, with their old school roots and their antiquated layout. Many hold a common ethnicity: Italian, Polish, Armenian, Indian, Chinese; budding towns that were once a haven to the world's transplants. Some are known for their politics, some for their crime. Some are home to a company's white-collar headquarters, and some house the manufacturing plants.

But over the years they've grown into each other, overlapping and mixing into new life forms. And all the while a special kind of transplant keeps moving in, those with no identity or tradition, those who can't identify with anything unless it's in the latest fashion magazine or television commercial. These people bring the chains with them: chain restaurants, chain clothing stores, chain coffee shops, chain movie theatres. They creep into each suburb one-by-one, supplanting what was once there, and then pull taut across the flat landscape. I don't know if these chains are keeping everything down or holding everything together.

Regardless, I'm not complaining. I myself am one of those transplants, one who didn't have any customs or traditions until they were defined for me. I didn't know what I liked or wanted until everyone else wanted it too. But since I've been living in a secluded section of Athens, the only change I must endure is the list of patients I treat. The television ads and mass marketing campaigns hold no sway over me. The clinic is where I should be; its idyllic pace and complete removal from the world soothe my troubled past.

But now that I can see the city rising up before me, I can feel the energy of a summer Friday in Chicago, the silent moment before the gates open and the dogs are let loose, to run as fast as they can, as hard as they can, into the great wide open, as if this weekend were really the start of a weeklong vacation, a summer break or an early retirement. The calling of complete and total freedom, which comes to an abrupt end on Monday morning. I turn up the stereo, step on the gas, and burn through suburbia, keeping an eye on the Sears Tower rising on the horizon, aiming for the heart of it all.

With the sun at our backs, the windows rolled down and the wind flapping past us into the backseat, each mile looks like another postcard, "Welcome to Chicago." We make our way onto Lake Shore Drive, merging through McCormick Place, the largest convention center in North America, and know thousands upon thousands more have also made this journey for a weekend in Chicago. Soldier Field, The Field Museum, Adler Planetarium, Shedd Aquarium, we pass each of these historic sites in a few minutes, trying to take them in as Lake Michigan opens up behind them, dotted with a few small boats and a single cargo ship off on the horizon. Farther up we pass Buckingham Fountain, the almost complete Millenium Park, and eventually exit Lake Shore as we see Navy Pier jutting out onto the lake, its oversized Ferris wheel turning like a gear between land, lake and sky.

We make our way to Wacker Drive and around to the Hyatt Regency, which overlooks the canyon of towers along the Chicago River, and has a massive bar above the lobby. But before heading up, we must drive four levels down a tightly wound ramp into the parking lot. Our windows are still open and the Mustang's wheels squeal as it gently works its way down.

"I hate these underground parking garages," Paige says.

"Me too," I say, "but think about how much parking would cost if they weren't underground."

"I know, but think of all the fumes. It's disgusting. I can taste it."

We were just outside, with the summer breeze coming off the lake, billowing around us, and now we're surrounded by a toxic smell as we burrow into the dark and deep bowels of the hotel. When we park, I put the stick in neutral and give the accelerator a quick short pump. The engine rumbles and echoes throughout the garage, its deep bass making the seats shake, and the fumes roil around us.

"Men," Paige says, "always having to prove their masculinity."

"Sorry," I reply, thinking about the power ready at the tap of a foot, controlled between my hands.

"All these cars spitting out their poison. I'm surprised anyone can survive down here."

"Actually," I correct, with knowledge I shouldn't have, "emission standards have gotten so high that one can't actually die from the exhaust of a new car."

"But an old beast like this…" Paige says.

"Yes," I nod, "an old beast like this…Sorry," I repeat, quickly putting the Mustang into park and turning off the engine. Paige thinks I'm sorry for revving the engine and letting this old car spit its poison around us, which I am, but that's not why I say it. I can taste the fumes more than ever, cough, and climb out of the car, wiping my eyes.

We grab our luggage, head to the elevator, and with the push of a button and a short wait up, emerge into the open hotel lobby where warm sunlight pours in from the surrounding windows, the putrid thoughts from the garage far behind us. This is vacation.

Paige looks up through the atrium, giving a half spin like a country girl taking in the big city. I notice the huge bar stretching across the other side, confirming that it matches what I read in the review. That may come in handy, I think. We check in and head up to the 14th floor, which looks down on the river below, lined in both directions by skyscrapers, like a moat with castle walls on both sides. "It's beautiful," Paige exclaims as she opens the curtains and leans against the glass, swiveling her view up and down the river.

It is, I think to myself. "So, what do you want to do now?"

"I don't know."

"We could go to a museum, do some shopping, or walk down to the lake? Whatever you want."

"Let's do it all."

"What about the Art Institute?" I suggest. Margaret and I used to go there quite often. I wasn't a big fan at first, intimidated, feeling like I should know something about art while Margaret kept pointing out details I would have never noticed or conjuring some art history fact I would have never studied. But as we kept coming back, it was the familiarity I liked, the comfort of knowing which gallery I was in, who the artists were and what piece would greet me around the corner. Margaret always seemed to have something new to say, some new theory or history or idea, which was so Margaret. I told her I had achieved the more Zen-like approach, taking it all in, feeling the art rather than describing it, and just being. Margaret didn't care for that answer. I enjoyed the art, and I enjoyed walking around while making snide little comments, but more than anything, I enjoyed holding Margaret's hand. That was art and that was the pleasure of just being.

And so we walk south, alongside the still-under-construction Millennium Park, even though we're already a few years into the new millennium. We reach the steps and proceed up between the entrance guards, two weathered lion statues, and I'm glad they have the decency and composure to not ask where Margaret is, because I'm not thinking about her at all.

Right before we drop into the building's shade, I look over and see the sun reflect off Paige's hair in a way I didn't expect, adding shine and texture, like the first rays of morning sun highlighting the small waves across a dark lake. I hold the door for her, pay our admission, and I lead her straight and up, toward *A Sunday on La Grande Jatte*, toward the comfort of familiarity, even though it's always bigger than I remember, and as we approach she nonchalantly takes my hand in hers.

For the next hour, we act like lovers. Not passionate, just two interlocking pieces, so if you asked any of the patrons how long we had been together, they would have said years, maybe decades. We move fast, agreeing we don't want to be here all day, but manage the familiar. *Paris Street; Rainy Day*, *Nighthawks*, *American Gothic*, *The Bedroom*, *The Old Guitarist*, *Wheatstacks*, *Wheatstacks*, and another *Wheatstacks*. Paige tells me what she likes and I tell her what I like, never bothering with how or why. She's matching my Zen appreciation, and sometimes when we stop she takes her other hand, reaches across her chest and touches my upper arm with her finger tips. Both hands on me. Art.

We also watch the children, some herded into large groups while others roam free, and we're more interested in their reaction to the art than our own, as if we're in that comfortable place in our lives, that comfortable place with each other where we can reminisce on innocence and how much we have grown since we were that age. We enjoy pretending like this, pretending everything is all right.

Eventually we look up and find ourselves at the exit, and with a nod of agreement, exit. We head north and things are going so smoothly that I'm surprised how hard the feeling hits me. As we walk away, I glance back at the museum and wonder if I'll ever be back. I notice the lion statue we just passed has the decency not to make eye contact, as I know what he's thinking. "Where's Margaret?" For a moment I think of the pictures I have at home, my own little "museum," and I remember one taken right on these steps, the three of us smiling after we asked some bystander to take our picture.

The feeling starts like déjà vu, but I know I've been here before and that it should feel familiar. I know what's the same, and more importantly, I know exactly what's different from my last visit. I know who's different. But then the stairs look like they're sliding, tilting to a frightening angle. The street angles away too, and the buildings curve and bend like blades of grass in the wind. I drop to a knee, hoping not to fall, and more importantly not to start tumbling down Michigan Avenue. I place my palm on the ground, steadying myself while trying to get a grip. Vertigo at ground level; if the street tilts any more I'll start falling down the street, falling a full, magnificent mile.

"What's wrong?" Paige asks.

"Nothing," I say calmly from my darkness. "Just a slight spinning feeling."

"Is it your head or your stomach?"

"Both."

She massages the back of my neck and I concentrate on that. "That feels good," I say, unable to get out anymore. I sit for a while, we sit, and I can tell Paige is worried. She asks a few more questions but I just nod my head that everything will be all right. Just as everything fell away, it starts coming back just as quickly; gravity correctly starts pulling down, steadying me against the hard concrete. Seat belts are fastened, tray tables are up, and soon I'll be back on the same ground with everyone else.

It's difficult to be back. It's difficult to be back and sober, as a drink will help prevent me from thinking about where I am, who I am, what I am. I could use a drink.

I then hear the first rumble of a jet engine passing overhead.

THE WHITE BARN

The craft room was large and wide-open, with engineered wood beneath, rafters high overhead, and large white walls packed with temporary art. Wide benches filled most of the space, where patients could spread out their materials. All sorts and skill levels were on display here. Some people drew pictures with crayons, simple stick figures and square houses, working in an art form that had no onus to impress. Others pasted pasta to pre-drawn pictures. Some used water color, some painted. One man, a true artist, sculpted an amazing bust of Vladimir Lenin. I asked him why he chose Lenin, and he told me he had difficulty sculpting hair. I wondered if his home was a gallery of the follicly challenged, Dwight D. Eisenhower, Mahatma Gandhi, Winston Churchill and Telly Savalas. Some of the doctors believed this meant something deeper, while I pictured a hairpiece placed atop each clay bust.

But the one thing almost everyone did, no matter the medium, was paint the white barn. The back wall of the craft room was all glass, and the view opened up to an old soybean field on a gently rising slope, topped by an old white barn, its paint falling off in flakes, revealing the weathered strain of age. This view was perfectly tranquil and really showed the patients how removed from the world they were, how they had found a fold in time and could now relax, reflect on their troubles without being pressured.

And because of this, everyone eventually drew or painted the white barn. We had easels just to the side of the window, dedicated for the patient who was ready to start their first or fiftieth recreation of the white barn. And when they were done, we hung them on the opposite wall, a collage of soy fields and white barns. On one side was the open window, revealing the perfect white barn, Plato's white barn, while on the other side hung everyone's rendered image, collective reflections on the cave wall.

At one point, the farmer who owned the barn almost tore it down. He said it was too old and too far from the main house for him to use. He wanted to build a new one, farther down the other side of the hill, and would plant crops where the white barn had been. The clinic's director told him how much the patients loved that white barn, how it represented their stay at the hospital. The farmer just shook his head, now resigned even more that taking it down was the right thing to do. He didn't like the idea of his property being eyed and ogled by a bunch of crazies, didn't like the thought of all those loony tunes watching him go in and out of his barn as if he were some exhibit at the loony zoo. But the hospital offered to pay him generously, not only for the land but for the barn's upkeep. With this, the farmer figured the crazies could do whatever they wanted, and if they wanted to pay him to maintain some old barn, well, their money was as good as anyone else's.

When I first started working at the hospital, the first time I worked in the crafts room, I thought how, rather than paint the white barn, it would be an interesting picture to turn an easel around and paint the white barns on the other side of the room. The white barn had little interest for me, at least when compared to the affect it had on others, the meaning it gave to them and how they tried to capture it. The white barn had become our art class's bowl of fruit, and to me, capturing everyone's rendition seemed more appealing than the actual subject.

The first patient I saw paint the art room wall of white barns was Harold Metcalf. He had painted the one outside half a dozen times, and many of those renditions now hung on the opposite wall, but he was the first patient I saw turn his easel around and make an attempt at the art inside the hospital. Over time, a few others did it, and that's when I began my hypothesis.

I'm sure it began out of vanity, since painting the back wall of white barns felt like my idea, and thinking it a smart thing to do, anyone else who came to this perspective must be intelligent too. I hypothesized that they would be the ones who got out early, overcame their burdens first, and once they did, were less likely to come back.

I didn't have a lot of data, but the few people who turned the easel did seem to follow this pattern. Harold Metcalf was close to leaving already when he first tried it. Maria Agravejo was only with us for seven days. John Dooley, Jimmy Schwartz and Patti Schweppe all had stays of less than three weeks and never came back. The only one who ever painted the wall of barns and did come back was Anna Tolaris, but she had so many issues that it would have been a near miracle for her to gain control over all of them in one fell swoop.

And then of course there was Przemek Korczowski. He arrived on a Saturday and that afternoon, during his first hour in the crafts room, he painted the wall of white barns. I remember thinking, "This guy won't be here for more than two weeks." I talked to his doctor, Doctor Lewis, who said Przemek was the type who answered everything with insight, explaining exactly what his answers meant as he said them, what moment in his past they sprouted from and which part of his psyche they came from. Doctor Lewis told me Przemek often joined group discussions, asking other patients questions that were more insightful, had more "psychiatric punch," then even his own.

Doctor Lewis also described him as being lonely. It seemed like he understood what was going on around him so well, what every action, feeling, motive and consequence meant, that he had trouble feeling connected to anything. My colleague thought his intellect and insight contributed to his depression, but I had hope they would help him find a way out. I thought anyone who could stop looking at the white barn outside, who could turn their attention around and see themself in the room, that was the person who could most help themself.

Even though my prediction was right, I was disappointed when Przemek checked himself out six days later. Wednesday afternoon, he said he was ready to leave, that he had a better understanding of who he was and was ready to go home. And since patients check themselves in, they can always check themselves out. The only power we have to keep them is if we think they might be a physical threat to themselves or others, which was a category Przemek did not fall into.

I was disappointed he left because in my mind, we both thought the same way, and so I wanted to get to know him better. And I didn't know what to think when I found out he drove three hours east that Wednesday afternoon, found a secluded beach entrance, loaded his pockets with rocks, and took a walk along the Atlantic's sandy bottom.

When I saw him paint the wall of white barns, I remember going up to him and saying, "Very insightful." He nodded, and I asked him if he had a name for it. He muttered "I'm trying," and at the time I thought he meant he was trying to come up with a name. But I now believe that was the name of his painting, *I'm Trying*.

THE SUN

"Let's walk a little," I say, once my panic attack or déjà vu or nausea or vertigo or whatever the hell it was passes. "We can do some window shopping," I add, trying to distract Paige.

"Are you sure you're all right?"

"Yeah, I'm fine," I say, heading toward Michigan Avenue at a brisk pace to substantiate that claim.

"You scared me," Paige says.

"Everything's fine," I lie, "I think I just need some food." I'm still full from my earlier gorging at the Cracker Barrel, but we stop at a deli and I get a small roast beef sandwich. Paige gets a bagel with veggie cream cheese.

"Better?" she asks.

"Much."

"So what's next?"

"I hear there's some good shopping around here." I take Paige by the hand and lead her back north, then east alongside the river, before crossing over. The weather is almost perfect, clear and sunny, with just a little too much humidity. "Let's stop for a drink," I suggest, pointing to the outside patio already filling up, with a view down along the river, able to watch the boats work their way up and down, the ferries filled with people taking the architectural tour, shielding their eyes as they gaze toward the heavens, their big cameras out and snapping away.

Paige orders a Chardonnay, not any particular one, and I get a Miller Lite, which sounds good in the heat. Last night's scotch was just a warm up, a light jog the day before the big race. The day before the marathon. This light beer, outside and enveloped in sunshine, is the first hundred meters after the gun goes off, an easy pace past the starting line, before the running crowd spreads out and I can start to find my pace. This is the first beer and I've got a long way to go. "Cin cin," I say to Paige, and we tap glasses and take our first sip. The beer tastes frighteningly good.

A boat horn bellows below us, delivering an unnecessarily deep, goose-like honk that excites the tourists on board. They look around and wave sorry, like they're the attraction and everyone is watching them. Paige waves at the boat and I smile. "Sometimes I just love this city," I tell Paige.

"Me too. I don't know why I don't come here more often."

"When was the last time you were here?""

"Oh, I don't know. Ten years ago? Maybe more. But it's not going to be that long until next time. How about you?"

"Me? It's been centuries since I've been here."

"Centuries? Like the World's Fair? Or was it the great fire that drove you out?"

"Okay, I'm exaggerating a bit. I was here last year. I come once a year, every year, but it feels like such a long time, like centuries. And yet..."

"And yet what?"

"And yet Chicago is my memory palace."

"Your what?"

"Memory palace."

"What's a memory palace?"

"Technically, it's a trick for memorizing things, especially long lists. People that count cards or memorize the phonebook, they usually use it. Basically you take a physical place you know and spread the things you're memorizing through the rooms. For some reason your brain can bring up what's next on the list if it's associated with a location you know. It's good for simpler things too, like memorizing anti-depressants and their side effects."

"So you've memorized a phonebook from Chicago? A phonebook of what, past girlfriends?"

"No, it's just an analogy. Part of the trick of a memory palace is when you can't remember what's next, you visualize going into the next room and suddenly there it is, conjured up whether you want it or not. I feel like that walking around here."

"So it's just a place with lots of memories?"

"Yes. It seems like every street corner conjures up a new memory."

"You can keep calling it a 'Memory Palace'," Paige says with air quotes, "if that makes you feel better."

"Thank you. So understanding."

"And what memory is this part of the palace conjuring, your highness?"

"Tough crowd," I say. My beer is half full. "Right now, not a specific memory. I remember walking across that bridge, the State Street Bridge, heading south to meet friends at a bar. Friday afternoon and just excited to get out. I once had a date over there." I nod at the outdoor café on the other side of the river. "It was a setup, and I quickly realized she had a thing for my friend who set us up. That didn't go anywhere, but she had nice eyes."

"Nice eyes?"

"Yes, nice eyes. That's not a euphemism either. And House of Blues, you can't see it but it's right around the corner. We saw Blues Traveler there. The Spin Doctors. Somebody else I can't remember. Good times, all."

"That's cool."

An anniversary dinner at McCormick and Schmick's. Three of us taking the architectural tour on the The First Lady. A trip up the Ferris wheel with dripping ice cream cones and no napkins. More good memories I won't mention. My beer is gone, and I nod to the waiter who asks if I want another.

"So," Paige says, "are you reminiscing these good times, and that's all, or are you also thinking, 'Where did the time go?'"

"Where did the time go?" I ask. "Or more exactly, I'm thinking, damn I'm old."

"I know that feeling. Wait until we are really old."

"I'm banking on senility."

"Lucky you."

"It must be kicking in already, as surely we're old friends, but sometimes I have the feeling we just met."

Paige raises her glass to me and my freshly replaced beer, "Paige," she says, "nice to meet you."

"The pleasure is all mine," I say, clinking my glass.

And the jets shoot by again, audible well before we see them, the sound swelling around us until it breaks overhead, visible for only a few seconds between the cracks in the skyline. "What is going on? Is there a military base nearby?" Paige asks.

"No."

"Then what's with all the jets?"

"The Chicago Air and Water Show is this weekend. The show is Saturday and Sunday, but their practice is today."

"Oh, that's so much better."

"Better than what?"

"I don't know, I just had a bad feeling, like there was another 9/11 or something."

Almost four years later, and that is still everyone's first thought. "No," I say, "we're safe." So safe that we have the most powerful jets in the world, and we use them to put on a show. Nothing bad could ever happen here.

We finish our drinks and continue walking, up toward the Magnificent Mile. We are out of place peering into the department store windows, staring up at the overhead buildings, walking slowly amidst the Chicago bustle while people cut around us, shaking their heads impatiently. But inside we fit right in, staring at displays, getting asked if we need help with anything, holding things up and checking price tags.

"Where are we going?" Paige asks, as I lead her southwest from Michigan Avenue.

"I believe there's a Nordstrom over here."

Paige doesn't protest. We enter to the sound of the grand piano being gently played by an older gentleman in a sport coat with elbow patches, and no one looks at him as we pass in our shorts and sandals.

"Is there anything you want to look for?" she asks me.

"No."

"I could spend all day here."

"Let's not go that far, but I don't mind watching you shop for a while."

And I don't. She walks through the racks, holding up blouses, dresses and various accessories to which I nod and say they look nice. A few I say no to, my least favorites, not that there's anything wrong with them. Never shrug your shoulders like you don't care. It's better to have an opinion, which shows you're paying attention.

"Really?" she asks on a few, and I just nod my head as if to say trust me, which for some reason she does.

I can't help admiring Paige's athletic figure, the way garments hang on her shoulders and draw into her waist. When she tries something on, her arms and hands move along it like a game show model's, accentuating what she has, even enhancing her form. She seems excited by a number of outfits, but looks at me questioningly too, hoping for affirmation. When I see her truly like something, I'll utter an authentic, "Wow!" The clear winner though is a sundress, a white one with a light floral print that hangs carelessly about her in a sensual manner. And even at the top, where it hangs loosely from her shoulders and displays the tendons in her neck, the tendons I found unattractive the night before, I now find I want to be near them. Young girls don't have tendons like these. They're the sign of someone getting older, still working out and looking great, but a little bit of the underlying structure is showing. I prefer that, a glimmer behind the façade, and I want to press my lips to her neck, between those cords that make up Paige, and breathe in the scent of her being. Of her being here, now, with me.

"You're going to wear that one out of here," I tell her. And though I'm sure she looked at the price tag while trying it on, she reaches around for it again, at which I grab her hand. "I'll get it."

"Oh no, you don't have to."

"No, I do. You look fantastic in that dress. It's worth it to me just to see you wearing it for the rest of the day."

She looks at me sweetly and gets on her tiptoes and hugs me, pressing against me as she holds herself up. This gives me a chance to breathe her essence, to actually hold it, and it is worth every penny, worth the white sundress, the baby blue blouse, the green top thingy and the tan skirt I buy for her. But I am tired of shopping, and as we leave I say, "Let's go somewhere for a drink."

We take a cab to the hotel, drop her new acquisitions and old clothes off at the room, freshen up, and head back out into a cab. "Melvin B's," I tell the cabbie, and a quick trip later, a breeze flowing in through the cracked windows, we're at the outdoor bar and café on State Street. It's mid-afternoon, and I'm fairly certain we have all the time in the world, hours and hours and hours, although the back of my mind reminds me that, when drinking, time can accelerate so quickly, like the propeller spin of a clock face in a bygone movie montage, not only signifying that time has passed, but that it passed in an instant.

Another plane flies overhead, not a jet but some sort of stunt plane with whirring propellers, and Paige asks, "Have you ever been to the air show?"

"A few times."

"Is it fun?"

"It's nice, but you need good company."

"What do you mean?"

"It's fun to watch, but it's an all-day event. Some planes fly overhead, do their stunts or whatever, and then it's fifteen or twenty minutes of downtime where you just wait. If you're not with interesting people, it can get pretty boring."

"Hmmm. I guess so."

"A lot of people throw parties though, open up their roof tops and what not. That's the best way to see it. I was at a pool party on the top of an apartment building, at North and Wells. That was awesome."

"How long did you live here?"

"Not sure. A long time. But it seems a long time ago."

"Damn you're old," Paige kids.

"I am," I say, "but it's not my age."

"What is it?"

I just don't know how I got here. I never expected the path I'd take, to become who I am. Whatever the hell that means. "Nothing," I say. "Just thirsty."

I take her hand, squeeze it, and let go. And she doesn't press me even though she wants to.

AUGUST, AGO

It was early morning, late summer, when the kitchen phone erupted down the hall. I had just stepped out of the shower into the withdrawn darkness before sunrise, still a bit groggy, when the silence was broken. I grabbed a towel and ran down the hall, not bothering to cover myself because no one else was up and I wanted to keep it that way. I managed to lift the receiver midway through the third ring, but instead of listening to whomever was calling, I intently listened to the sounds in our condo to see if anyone had awoken. "Sorry for calling so early," said my boss, Nancy Morales, on the line. I was supposed to meet Nancy and a few other colleagues in Rosemont later that morning for a conference. I was up early to beat the traffic. The presenters, Nancy explained, had planned on flying in from New York last night, but due to airplane problems or something, spent most of the night on the tarmac and couldn't get another flight. The presentations were cancelled, which I didn't care about anyway, but the important part was she told me to take the day off and make it a three day weekend. The rest of what she talked about, our presenters' failed trip, the logistics of when we would make it up, a paper I was supposed to read or present or something, all kind of blurred together as I said, "Uh-huh" a few times, maybe a, "Thanks" while hanging up, as I realized I had an open day with nothing scheduled.

I properly wrapped the towel around me, wondering what I would do next as I put ground coffee into the machine. Instead of pressing the 'start' button, I went into the bedroom and slipped on some boxer-briefs, running shorts, a t-shirt and sat on the bed to slide on my socks.

"Who called?" the lump in the bed asked.

"Morales. They cancelled the conference. I've got the day off."

"How come?"

"Mechanical issues with their plane, bad weather, delays at O'Hare, something, maybe mad cow disease, I don't care. I've got the day off."

"Come back to sleep," Margaret said. She turned away from me, not for any reason but to readjust. For Margaret, sleeping in was like found treasure; she didn't understand how anyone could pass it by.

"Too late. I'm already up. Going for a run. I'll make breakfast when I get back."

I'm not sure exactly where I ran, probably my usual route to the North Avenue Bridge and along Lake Michigan. I think I put in four miles, the right distance to feel like I ran but not enough to feel spent. Margaret was still asleep when I returned, so I drank a Gatorade, started the coffee maker, and pulled out a mixing bowl, cast iron skillet and all the ingredients for my morning specialty. Margaret said I liked cooking in cast-iron to feel more like a man in the kitchen, and though I never admitted it, she was right. Every time I grabbed our skillet's stubby handle, my wrist stiffened, unprepared for the weight, and I thought back to those Tom and Jerry cartoons where someone was stopped in their tracks by the thwap of a skillet. Once you hold one, you know it's not hyperbole.

With everything measured, mixed and poured, I slid the skillet into the oven, set the timer, and with perfect synchronization heard the first sounds of play from down the hall. Our condo layout, front to back, was the front room that opened into the kitchen, Evelyn's bedroom, a small bathroom off the hall, and then our bedroom. Evelyn had just moved out of her crib into a bed, and rather than listening for her talking or crying and knowing she was still safe in her crib, we now listened for her playing, talking and exploring, a not quite two-year-old with free reign.

I opened her door and looked at her on the floor, sitting with a block in each hand, placing them on the head of her large stuffed unicorn, giggling as she released them and they fell onto the smaller stuffed animals gathered around. She didn't notice me, and though I should have watched her longer, unnoticed, I muttered, "Boo." Evelyn turned toward me, falling awkwardly onto her side, catching herself with her hands. "Evie baby," I said. (Not pronounced like Ee-vee, but Ev-ee, where the Ev sounds like the beginning of Everlast and Everbeautiful. Sorry, but people always called her Evie with that harsh leading E like in Adam and Eve, and it always bothered me. It's Evie, as in 'They lived happily ever after. That's her name.)

This day is important to me. I've thought about it many times, and the strange thing about memories is some fade while others grow stronger. Like waves on the beach, you're aware of them but can't distinguish one from the other, until that one that catches you just right, splashes high and gets you wet or almost knocks you over; that's the one you remember, that's the one you talk about. In a way it represents all those other waves, and as your memory of the others fade, this one becomes increasingly significant. This day was a perfect wave.

Evie regained her balance and stood just as I snatched her up, snuggled her against my sweaty shirt and kissed her soft curls. "Da-da," she said.

"Evie, want a Dutch Puff?"

I carried her to the kitchen and set her down on the strip of tile between counters, resting myself against the oven door. Evelyn knew which two drawers she could play in, the one full of diapers she could pull out and throw around, the other full of Tupperware that Evelyn liked to stack and knock over. Margaret always washed the plastic bowls when Evie was done, but I just put them back into the drawer. For a half hour she played in the drawers and climbed over me. When the timer went off I got up, grabbed an oven mitt and placed Evie far from the oven so I could pull out the skillet, inhaling the perfect dome of golden batter. A toothpick came out clean, and I placed breakfast on the stove to cool.

"I love that smell," Margaret said, entering the kitchen.

"Dutch Puff?" I asked, inhaling the scent of cinnamon and vanilla sugar filling the kitchen.

"Yum," Margaret said eying my creation on the stove, "but there's nothing like freshly brewed coffee."

"Mommy!" Evelyn shouted.

"My Evelina!" Margaret lifted Evelyn, perched her against a hip and gave her a kiss, making Evelyn believe she had all of Margaret's attention, while Margaret's other hand grabbed a coffee cup, filled it, and stirred in a splash of creamer. I'm pretty sure Margaret could hold Evelyn in one hand and build a house of cards with the other. She wore her tattered DePaul Blue Demon t-shirt and cornflower blue sleeping pants. Her dark hair was pulled back into a ponytail, and she looked up at me through an old pair of burnt red glasses she'd wear until she put her contacts in. She had no make-up on, but with her high cheekbones, thin nose, and gracious smile, was just beautiful. She was strong, kind and secure, just the type of woman I always dreamed of making coffee for, of sharing a marquee with in the Mommy and Daddy show.

"Evelina, Daddy has the day off. Is he going to ruin all the fun we had planned today?"

"Ruin your fun?" I asked. "Evie, Daddy IS the fun."

"Oh, really? And what's Daddy got planned for us, after he showers?"

"Stinky Daddy's going to eat first, then he's going to mow the lawn, and then he'll shower. After that, we're going to the park, and after that we're going to catch the Cubs game."

"Well, Mommy stands corrected. Maybe Daddy is fun after all."

"Did you hear that Evie? Mommy just said that Daddy's right and she's wrong."

Margaret lifted Evelyn and held her nose to nose for affect, "Daddy's so silly. Silly, silly Daddy. Mommy's never wrong."

That's us. Mommy and Daddy. We don't call each other that when friends are around, but when it's just the three of us we say it all the time. I used to make fun of a friend who was raised by his grandparents. They called each other Ma and Pa. How good of a relationship could you have with someone you called Ma? But I was in junior high then and didn't know much of anything. At some point you earn a title that's the most important title you'll ever have in your life, and if the person you live with is willing to keep calling you that, why not? Back then I thought Ma and Pa sounded like you were talking to your Ma and Pa, but it really means we're a mother and a father. Together. That's our role, and I was and always will be Daddy.

"Daddy's silly? You mean Daddy's funny," I corrected. "Daddy's the funnest, Mommy."

I'm not saying we would have called each other Mom and Dad forever, but definitely longer.

For the first two summers I was in college, I returned home and worked at the Park District. The Director of Parks attended my father's church and gave me the best job, riding lawn mowers. There were two models that I switched between. The first was the giant mower that we could drive down the major streets, big enough to compete with the other cars and fast enough to not be a complete nuisance, although most cars would dart around when there was an opening. This orange behemoth had wings that lowered when we got to our destination, three rotating blades on each, and was able to cut a wide swath at high speeds. That mower could do about anything. A football field in a half hour. The soccer fields and band shell around Centennial in a few hours. There weren't enough open fields to keep this monster busy all week, although I wished there were, as it was the best job and it was mine.

I also worked with the follow-up crew, which had three riding lawn mowers much like the ones people kept at home. They were used to trim what the largest mower couldn't reach, mainly a few laps around all the structures, the tennis courts, the playgrounds, the lakes, and the small parks spread out around town. We'd go out in a crew of three, maneuvering along back-roads to get from park to park, stopping to do figure eights like a Shriner's parade. That was a pretty good job too.

There was a third crew of push mowers and weed-whackers, who did real work, returning sweaty and grimy after toiling all day in the hot sun. I only joined this crew a few times, just enough to help me appreciate how sweet it was on the riding mowers.

I loved mowing with the behemoth. Sitting beneath the broiling sun, sipping from a water bottle and having no responsibility besides tracing the narrow line that separated the cut and uncut grass. Back-and-forth, back-and-forth. Of course it got boring, but you could drive up to a large park after a week of rain, with dandelions sprouting amidst thick tufts of grass, and within an hour or two look back and see nothing but a clean sheet of soft green earth, the type meant for throwing a Frisbee across while barefoot. As trivial as it really was, you felt like you accomplished something. I always enjoyed that scene in *Forrest Gump* when the city officials gave him the prestigious job of mowing the high school lawn, and you were supposed to laugh at him for taking it. But after having other jobs, real jobs, I looked back and realized riding a lawn mower was one of the best jobs one could ever have. As long as you didn't care about money, of course, just like Forrest.

I became a bit compulsive about mowing the lawn. When we had the middle floor of a three story condo, I volunteered to take care of the small swatch of grass out back, about six feet wide and twenty feet deep. I went out to the back deck and pulled an old push reel mower out of the thin storage shed, a rusted out hunk of metal I got at a garage sale for fifteen bucks. With a little oil and a blade sharpener, I restored it to a workable condition. Forward, turn, back, turn, repeat, repeat, repeat, five times up and five times down, and I was done. About ten minutes and the lawn was mowed. I enjoyed every one of those ten minutes. Barefoot.

I showered, Margaret got Evelyn ready, and we headed out to Webster Park, four blocks away. Margaret and I both carried coffee in our to-go cups, sipping away, and heating up our insides before the August sun would broil our outsides. The baby supplies were stuffed into an almost stylish, masculine diaper bag, which I carried over my shoulder. Margaret pushed the Peg Perego stroller with cup holder, and we did our best to be yuppies with the day off. Margaret would scoff at being labeled "yuppie" as she always claimed to be more a part of the counter-culture, although that wasn't really true. She was a photographer and though very skilled at her art, she made her money taking portraits of babies and children. She had a thing for strange art (not abstract, I told her, just downright strange), unknown bands and a pretty far left political tilt, but otherwise she was just as yuppie as the rest of us. Good food, expensive wine, nice clothes and a knack for thinking you were unique.

"Love you, babe," she said, and I glanced over to see if she was talking to me or Evelyn, and caught her staring right at me.

I smiled and inhaled my coffee, tempted to tell Margaret just how much I loved her, but just replied, "You too, babe." This wasn't a moment I look back on with regret. She knew I loved her; there was never any doubt.

"Can we get a few in the empty lot?" Margaret asked.

"I'm not working. We can do whatever you want."

Margaret had gotten her first digital SLR when Evelyn was born, the Nikon D1x, and carried it with her everywhere. This is why I carried the diaper bag. Her camera bag, lenses and flash were stuffed under the stroller. The empty lot, surrounded in part by a chain link fence, full of weeds and debris, had a single large ash tree blossoming in the back corner. We had taken pictures here before, and I think Margaret liked the grittiness of it, sometimes framing the fence or the graffiti on the adjoining condos, but almost always getting the ash tree. She preferred this location over the plastic rainbow backdrop of the park; not that we didn't also have a million pictures at the park.

Twenty pictures here, twenty pictures there, a few in the morning, a few before Evie went to bed, and suddenly we had what seemed like a billion shots of Evelyn. When Margaret had a job and was taking pictures of someone else's kids, she was always sure to take some test shots of Evelyn first. Where was the light coming from? Were there any shadows to work with? Where was the best place to compose the scene? Could she use a fixed lens and open it up, or would the zoom give her more flexibility? (The answer was always to use the fixed lens, but Margaret pretended she might use the zoom.) *Stand here Evelyn. Evie, sit on this stool I brought. Hold this empty frame and smile. Now turn the frame.* Every sitting Margaret took of someone else's kids began with a plethora of Evelyn shots, shots the clients would never see, but Margaret would put into her 'Library of Evelyn.'

"The sun's already a little harsh," Margaret said, surveying the lot we already had a million pictures of. She didn't mean the heat, but the light's edges, the way it quickly transitioned from light to shade, without a smooth blend. Cloud cover was ideal, and there was only a solitary puff on the horizon.

"Evie could stand in the shadow and you could use your fill flash thingy," I said, having picked up a few tricks of the trade.

"Yeah, but let's make this quick. These'll make for good black and whites. How about have her stand over there. Do you want to sit beside her?"

"Sure," I said, sitting on the ground, forcing a natural smile like I've been told; a few shots while looking at the camera, a few looking away. "Let me get you two," I suggested, and Margaret and I switched positions. She made sure the camera was set up correctly, pointed to the shutter button as if I hadn't taken a few thousand pictures myself. Five minutes and we were done. Evelyn no longer cried or whined about having her picture taken. She knew it made Momma happy, and that made Evie happy too.

Webster Park had some plastic jungle gym structures, a plastic turtle to climb on, two slides and six swings, all outlined with benches for parents and nannies to congregate while keeping watch. Margaret greeted the ones she knew, the one's whose kids played with Evie, and I sat back and watched for a while. I chased Evie around the jungle gym. I reached up through the slats alongside the bouncy bridge and tried to tickle her until she put her foot down, "No Dad-die!" I laughed and returned to my park bench.

Margaret put Evie on a swing and pushed her while talking to another mom we had met out for drinks and appetizers earlier that year. I couldn't remember her name, wasn't sure if I ever knew it, and only referred to her as Austin's mom. They both held coffee cups in one hand, rhythmically pushed with the other, and talked about who knows what. I watched and saw as Austin kicked his foot out, managing to make contact with Evelyn's leg as she swung backwards. It couldn't have hurt, but with every push and every pass Austin tried to kick her again and Evelyn's face scrunched up with fear. "Down," she said, "down, down!" but Margaret casually told her to wait a minute while she finished her conversation. It was no big deal, but I got up and walked over to Evelyn, grabbed her at the apex of her forward swing, lowered her back down and lifted her out.

"Dad-die!" she screamed, pressing her red chubby cheek against mine and squeezing the back of my neck. "Austin kicked me," she whispered.

"I know," I said, and gave him a stern glance that melted his devious little smile. Nobody fucks with my little girl, I thought, carrying Evelyn away and laughing at myself for mentally swearing at a four year old. For the next ten minutes Evelyn sat on my lap and talked to me. I don't remember anything she said, but she played with my wedding ring, squeezed my cheeks and talked to me. For ten minutes I was her whole world, and she mine.

Later that morning, we went back to the condo, fed Evelyn, restocked our baby supplies, and then caught the Red Line up to Wrigley. Along the way I heard a low rumbling noise, long and deep, but the train car was crowded and loud and I didn't think much about it. There were a few more similar noises, distant swoops of hurtling air that seemed to catch other people's attention, but I was enthralled in my own little familial bubble. We made our way around Murphy's Bleachers, which was packed with drinkers, scalped tickets under the El tracks, and then made our way to the upper deck behind third base, which was far away from the action but also meant we wouldn't have the sun in our eyes. We weren't quite too old to sit in the bleachers with the fresh-out-of-college drunks, at least we didn't think we were, but Evelyn was definitely too young.

The vendors came by and we got two hot dogs, two pretzels, nachos with cheese and an Old Style, then piled it all at our feet as we stood for the national anthem. The Cubs were second-to-last in their division, playing the last place Brewers, and the game wasn't anything more than a chance to sit outside and talk without awkward silences. It wasn't about winning or losing; it was about having a game to watch. As the song ended and the crowds began to sit, a rumble rose up from the south. Someone with headphones shouted, "Holy Cow!" probably echoing the sentiments of Harry Carray on WGN. There was a moment of confusion, a concerned look toward Margaret as I picked Evelyn up again, and then it happened. A fighter jet flew over Wrigley Field, low and tight, cutting a deep bellow across the light blue sky, holding the crowd noise in check as it passed. After a pause and a brief moment of astonishment, the crowd erupted.

Evelyn clapped her chubby hands and screamed, laughing so hard I could feel her rocking in my arms. I suddenly remembered the Air and Water Show was that weekend, where jets and bi-planes and all sorts of cool stuff would be streaking across Lake Michigan, and they had their practice today before the big show tomorrow. Those sounds I heard on the El were jets performing their soaring aerials above the city. Something cool had happened and we were all part of it. I hope Evelyn felt it, that momentary sense of being awestruck, that the world was an amazing place and you were lucky to be part of it. I hoped she would always remember that moment.

With Evie by my side, I was also excited by this show I had casually dismissed in years past. I was part of something too, shouting, "Woo-hoo!" with the cheering crowds while watching Evelyn laugh. I knew I was part of something, and I assumed it would last forever.

We left the game early so Evie could get her nap in. I don't remember if the Cubs were winning when we left, and I doubt I ever looked to see who won. It didn't matter; I had a great time. Evie napped at home while Margaret and I put together a wine rack from Ikea. When Evie woke we played games, read to her, got Penang's chicken pad thai delivered, and ate our favorite meal while Evie mouthed cut-up chicken nuggets. We laid in Evie's room and, while Margaret read, Evie's head floated slowly down against my chest until she fell asleep. I lifted her over her bed and, with the caution of a bomb diffuser, carefully lowered her down onto her mattress, slipped my hands out and waited, not breathing, ready to wrap her back in my arms at the first outburst. Evie's eyes opened and we froze, but with the knowledge her Mommy and Daddy were watching over her, they drifted shut again and she was out.

With Evie down we opened a bottle of Cabernet Franc, watched a romantic comedy I could never name, and fell asleep on the couch. I awoke just before midnight and spent a minute looking around, wondering where I was, piecing together how I got there and what happened that day. I nudged Margaret and watched her do the same, then the two of us ambled back to the bedroom, baby-monitor in tow, and crawled into bed. With my ear pressed into the pillow, I opened one eye to watch the alarm clock tick past midnight. The day was over and I was happy, yet I had no comprehension that the best day, the very best day of my entire life, had just passed.

IRONY

Paige and I reach Melvin B's, which is abuzz with people. Most of the seating is outside, each table packed full and the space in between jammed with more people, enjoying a warm Friday afternoon in the city, beautiful people with their drinks in hand, looking around at all the other beautiful people. Waitresses pry through the masses taking orders, small girls with large trays held high as they weave back and forth through the crowd. The auburn-haired hostess with a nose ring stops talking to the bouncer long enough to let us know there is an hour-long wait for a table. I nod and slip her a twenty and she says she'll see what she can do.

I'm not the type of guy who slips money to hostesses, but I have been here before with people who do, and I can mimic their behavior. Melvin B's is for the young business people who think they deserve an afternoon off, who feel a happy hour out in the sun is the perfect way to start the weekend, rounding out their thirty-hour workweek. They all want to congregate with similar minded people, to talk and laugh and figure out who they know and how much money they make and who has the best condo.

There are a few hotbed tables here too, the centers of attention. One is a group of girls, probably strippers, drinking brightly colored drinks and smoking away, holding out their fake hair, fake breasts, fake lips, fake eyelashes, fake tans, fake anything and fake everything, knowing everyone is watching them as they look out occasionally to bask in the stares and perhaps make fun of someone. Another table is all guys, leaning back in their chairs, everyone pushed away from the table as if the people standing around weren't already pressed shoulder to shoulder. They are muscular, talk loud, and like to high-five each other, shout profanities and make other big movements that draw attention. There are a few other groups trying to make their scene, but these are the two that stand out as the hostess leads Paige and me through the crowd to a small table for two against the wall.

As the hostess paves our way, I notice one of the girls from the stripper table looking at me. I nod, unable not to glimpse at her fake bosom pressing out from a tight yellow wrap. She's old too, and if she's not an ex-stripper she's an old stripper, nature putting up a fight on her silicon-enhanced chest. But she's still got herself done up, and she's at a table with girls closer to their prime, girls that everyone is looking at, and I look away while she's still smiling and sit down across from Paige. This isn't the Cracker Barrel anymore, and nobody's looking at Paige thinking she's the best-looking one here. But she is attractive. And my vanity is creeping back from somewhere, so I need to remind myself that I don't really care.

"You know what I want to do tonight?" she asks.

"What?"

"Go dancing."

"Hmmm."

"You don't like dancing?"

"No, I can dance. I just need a little something to loosen me up."

"A little liquor for your legs?"

"A lot of liquor. What kind of dancing do you like?" I am worried she's going to say Country Western or line dancing or something like that where I won't know a single song or step.

"Techno," Paige says, and I'm not sure whether to be relieved or not. Better than country, but I don't know what I'm doing there either. Actually, there's not a single kind of dancing I'm good at, and at least with techno we'll be jam-packed into a dark room where nobody will really have any 'moves.'

Our waitress makes her way to our table and Paige orders a Cosmopolitan while I order a vodka gimlet. Vodka with a splash of Rose's lemon juice. Nothing's better when sitting out in the sun.

"Have you ever been to Division Street?" Paige asks. "I've gone dancing there before and had fun."

"Oh yeah, I know exactly where that is." She doesn't realize that the street we're on, State Street, intersects with Division about two blocks north, and the bars she wants to go to are right there. Paige doesn't know Division Street is generally snubbed by people who live in Chicago and caters more to out-of-towners and suburbanites who drive in for a night. People like us.

And then I hear my name. "Holy shit," the approaching stranger calls out, "I thought that was you." A burnt-faced Andrew McCarran makes his way through the crowd, half stumbling into people as he holds his lowball glass up high to avoid spilling. "What the fuck are you doing here?"

"Hey, hey McCarran," I say, extending my hand. He walks past it and hugs me. I feel his drink spilling down my back, his breath emanating pure alcohol, and yet I'm thankful for the hug. I've always liked McCarran. Everyone likes McCarran.

"Fucking great to see ya."

"Thanks. You too."

"What the hell? I didn't hear you were going to be in town or anything."

"It's for some work stuff I have to do."

"What, a conference or something? Get together and talk about your crazies? A crazy conference?"

"If that were the case you surely would have been invited."

Andrew's drunk. Really drunk. As always. He's puffy too, no longer the fresh-faced day trader who was young and wild and letting off steam, but the seasoned commodity trader who's full of stories, filling the pit during slow times with tales of debauchery that the younger kids could only aspire to. Back in the day I would have done my best to catch up, really catch up, but now I just smile amicably and nod in agreement, throwing out small talk.

"So what are you up to?" I ask.

"Running the same racket, as always. Still at Goldman, but thought it was too nice a day to work all afternoon. Some of the guys from the pit and I decided to head here after the markets closed and have a few cocktails, catch some sun and watch the ladies."

Somehow it is almost 6:00, and I believe the markets closed three or four hours ago. McCarran could do a lot of damage in a few hours. Most people wouldn't make it out until at least seven or eight, after work, dinner, and a moment to unwind. McCarran was drunk by mid-afternoon, by the time the normal drunks started coming out. But he would also keep going strong through midnight, sometimes making it to sun up. He'd start with some work friends, and whoever could keep up would stay out, as they'd either meet people in the bar or meet up with a new shift of friends. He'd be on his cell, calling people at work and yelling at them to get the hell out of there because it was too nice a day to be working. He'd call them at home and slur a long message on their answering machines. He'd walk up to a table of girls and start a conversation, harmlessly talking and making them laugh until a few tables were joined together, all connected haphazardly through Andrew McCarran. As always, he was the life of the party. The self-titled Chi-Town Hustler. The Mick Mac Daddy McCarran.

And for that, for remembering good times without guilt, it is good to see him. But remembering is seldom a guilt-free process.

"So are you still working down in, uh…"

"Georgia?" I finish. "Yes."

"And that's going cool?"

"I enjoy it."

"Yeah, I'm still trading and all, same old thing."

At this point he notices Paige and extends his hand, "Hi there, I'm Andrew, Andrew McCarran."

"Hi. Paige," she says, "Nice to meet you."

And there's a pause.

I say she's a friend of mine from downstate.

And there's another pause.

McCarran looks from her to me with an eye of sympathy, not because of who Paige is, but who Paige is not.

And now I'm not sure what to do.

It's amazing how two opposing conditions can exist so close together. The fact that McCarran feels pity for me, reinforces that we were once friends. I've never seen him sad about anything, never seen him pause in a conversation or act uncomfortable. And now that he does, I'm glad, because it emphasizes that we were friends, and I almost want to put my arm around his shoulder and thank him for it, thank him for once being a friend. But I also have an urge to tell him to fuck off, tell him how dare he feel pity for me, that he's a stumbling drunk who's probably going to be wasted and alone at this stupid little bar forty years from now, if he's alive at all.

I want to tell him both things, but split the difference and tell him nothing.

So I look around uncomfortably myself. Above the bar is a hotel, if that's the right word. It's a beaten down hole where someone can stay a few weeks or a few months for next to nothing. It's for those with next to nothing. I've seen the people who stay there as they come and go out the side door, transients and vagabonds with little more than the shoes on their feet. Yet below, there's a beer garden that caters to the socialites of Chicago, gathered together to admire each other's looks, each other's style, each other's life. I wonder what those boarders think in their tiny, filth-ridden rooms, listening to the buzz of conversation below, perhaps taking a peak outside, wondering how everything can be so close to them, yet so far.

I wonder if it makes sense to them.

And further down State Street is Division, which has the bars where Paige wants to dance. A half-mile west on Division is Cabrini Green, the worst public housing debacle in the city, perhaps in the country. Plain, sixteen-story towers, packed to the gills with the poor of Chicago. Elevators that don't work and air-conditioners that never worked, just unit after unit stacked sideways and vertical and going on for blocks. Buildings that had been let go in the worst possible way, packed with dirt and grime, fires and garbage, and crime and more crime.

Meanwhile the rich have been building their houses closer and closer, until now Cabrini Green is surrounded on all sides with new condos and townhomes, expensive brick row houses getting bought up as quickly as they can be built, picture perfect streets with picture perfect homes, and all of them a stone's throw from Cabrini. The rich and the poor, living side by side, pretending the other isn't there, trying to ignore the extremes that are possible in life, the extremes that inexplicably buttress against each other.

Ironies. Confusions. Head-scratchers. The one that's always gotten me wasn't too far from here, at Prentice Hospital. Each floor was filled with the sick and the dying: cancers, heart attacks, car accidents and kidney failures inhabit room after room, but there is always that one floor that is dedicated to the maternity ward. This is where life begins, the most joyous event for everyone involved, and it takes place wedged between the last rites of the dying. Welcome to the world, but remember, you'll be back.

I remember when my father had intestinal cancer, going to Rush-Presbyterian every day to watch his decay. I'd get in the elevator with people like me, polite and quiet, coming in the morning wondering if their loved one made it through the night, leaving in the evening wondering if they had their last visit, if those final words were enough. But I'd also ride the elevator with those going to the maternity ward, friends and family with balloons, gift bags and stuffed animals that had "Congratulations" or "It's a Boy" printed in bold letters. And those people would try to contain their joy, stunting their conversation and offering up a sympathetic nod while they stood in the elevator beside us in mourning. I wonder if they realized how lucky they were to be at the hospital welcoming a birth rather than awaiting a death.

I couldn't blame them, but it confused me how we could end up enclosed, side by side, counting the numbers lighting above the doors, waiting. I knew one day they would be here under the same circumstances I was, probably already had, but I wondered when I would be able to come here under the opposite guise, when I would be able to celebrate life.

And through the silence, McCarran thinks of something to say. "Hey," he starts awkwardly, "Bill and Karen, they're having their annual party tomorrow, during the Air and Water Show."

"Really," I say. "They're still doing that?"

"Yep. It's become quite a tradition."

"Are they're still on what, Larrabee?"

"They moved a block over, to Cleveland. One of those three flats with a rooftop. It's right next to the El. You should go."

"Okay," I say with absolutely no intention of attending, "I just might."

And that gives us a break, the possibility that we will see each other tomorrow, so we don't have to try and force a catch up that neither of us wants.

"Excellent," says McCarran, shaking my hand. "I'll see you there." He nods to Paige as he scurries off, making a loud commotion of noise and jokes as he approaches his table across the beer garden.

"Who's that?" Paige asks.

"An old friend."

"There's something you're not telling me."

I take her hand and look at her seriously, as if to say I'm not trying to be a smart-ass. "There are a lot of things I'm not telling you, but they're all in the past. I'd rather not get into it now."

"You used to live here, right?"

"In the past," I say, hoping she'll leave it there.

"How long ago?"

"Ages ago."

"Why'd you move away?"

"Ages ago," I repeat.

"What does that mean?"

"I don't know," I say truthfully. "I just really don't want to get into it."

"What about that party tomorrow?"

"Oh no, I'm not up for that."

"Then what are we going to do?"

"We can go down to the lake front if you want to watch the show. Or we can go to one of the street fests. There are a million things to do in Chicago in the summer." And I let go of her hand and look around some more. The ex-stripper, or old stripper, is looking at me again.

"I liked the way you were so secretive at first," says Paige, "but now…"

"I know," I say. I have to smile at her again, because it's not my fault if she liked me for being mysterious. She's probably fallen for fifty guys before me because she thought they were quiet and mysterious, only to find out they're assholes. By now she should know. And yes, I know that whole writing in a bar and talking cryptic is my fault, but I just don't feel guilty, because I've known from the beginning, as much as I may try, there's nothing mysterious about me. In my mind, the rock's been kicked over and the earthworms and centipedes can be seen plain as day. "I'll make you a deal. I'll explain the whole thing to you when the time comes."

"You mean you'll explain it to me when you explain it to me?"

"Uh, yeah."

"Thanks."

And I realize they're playing a song I like, from a few years back, say maybe ten or fifteen years ago, a cheesy song with a good beat that got played at all the weddings of all my friends. But I'm tired of the past, tired of talking about it and tired of thinking about it, so I grab Paige and start dancing with her right there. Nobody else is dancing, so we look out of place. But Paige can move, and even though I can't, I look happy and confident and not too awkward, which is a dancing style that puts me above most guys. We spin around one table and then another, bumping people as we go, but everyone enjoys our merriment. We're showing off just as much as anyone, playing the game of one-upsmanship and becoming the center of attention for a brief moment, and then the song ends and we sit down and everyone turns back to their own circle, wondering why everyone's not looking at them.

EVERYTHING FALLS APART
WHEN YOU LEAVE FOR THE BATHROOM

I'm drunk.

We get a platter of mini-burgers and shoestring fries at Melvin B's, but I only eat two of them and let Paige have the rest. It's not enough for either of us, but the afternoon turned into evening and the crowds walking up and down State Street have transformed from the working class to the drinking class, heading out for a night of debauchery, and we decide to follow suit.

We leave and go north to Division Street, where Paige knows the bars to dance in, and start out at The Tavern. This is the only bar on the block filled with people our age, who stand around and socialize, most of whom have children at home and an ex or two in their pasts. But we're not up for acting restrained or civilized, and head next door to Bar Chicago, where a line of kids wait, standing in anticipation of the disco lights and thumping music that pour out from the windows above. We wait too, pay cover, and walk into a giant room packed wall to wall with young grinding bodies. I think this is what Paige wants, to act young, and so I buy another round of drinks and we work our way into the thicket.

With the lights and the speakers pounding, along with my head, things move fast. We're sweating amongst a thousand other sweating bodies, and I just glimpse flashes of arms and bellies and hair and asses all shaking to the music. Paige and I press against each other because we want to and we have to. We shout at each other now and then and laugh, never hearing each other but assuming something smart or funny was just said. And we make out right there, during a song, while nobody seems to notice or care that the two old folks are going at it on the dance floor. I'm fairly certain Paige tells me she likes me, even though I've been mysterious and holding back on her, she really likes me. I shout something back she can't hear and kiss her again, a long, slow, no-more-dancing-because-we're-kissing, kiss, and then we're back to dancing like nothing's changed.

We dance some more with that wonderful sense of togetherness, that sense of belonging that is always fleeting, that if I try and acknowledge it by saying something profound will only result in something awkward and stupid and the moment will be lost. And time goes by as the night gets longer and somehow a waitress keeps finding us in the middle of the dance floor, and I keep tipping her big and drinking more until I eventually tell Paige I have to go to the bathroom. And she's perfectly comfortable to wait right there, dancing alone, waiting for me.

As I make my way towards the back, looking for some sort of sign, I can't help thinking about Paige and our relationship. She must think we're working towards something meaningful, trying it out, and I feel like I've somehow agreed. I find a stairwell that rises along the back wall and leads to a balcony that surrounds the dance floor. When I get to the top, I see the ex-stripper or old stripper dancing with her friends and smiling at me once more. So I walk up to her big hair and big lips and big breasts and start dancing with her, above the crowds below, above Paige on the dance floor by herself, above the young boys below who can't keep their eyes off strippers. I start kissing this ex-stripper, or old stripper, not having spoken a single word to her yet, and she kisses me back, and I don't even think about Paige waiting patiently below.

I don't think about the fact that she was willing to take a chance and follow me on a whim and a promise of a good time. I don't think about how we had a really good day together, that she makes me laugh, that she's smart, or that she's kind. I don't think about her at all. I just make out with the ex-stripper, or old stripper, until she stops making out with me and turns and starts dancing with her friends, laughing as if I were no longer there. I stand there for a moment, watching these girls dance with their backs to me, and know the ex-stripper or old stripper got everything she wanted from me, and I got everything I wanted from her.

I really have to use the bathroom now. I eventually find one downstairs, back on the main dance floor, and stand in a hallway amid a line of guys all annoyed that they have to take this break to urinate, wishing they could avoid this inconvenience, wishing they were above it somehow. But me, I know this is where I belong, that right now I'm nothing more than a finely wrapped receptacle of piss and shit and blood and bile, nothing more than the most vulgar and disgusting elements held in such a deceptively clean vessel that everyone forgets what's inside. But I know, and I can smell it when I enter the bathroom, and I can feel its heat when I stand over the urine filled trough and piss on the back wall.

I check myself once in the mirror, to make sure the wrapping is still all right, thankful that I can use it to hide not only from others, but from myself. I stumble back to the main dance floor. But lots of things can happen while you're in the bathroom. Paige is nowhere to be found, and as I wander around I run into the ex-stripper or old stripper again, who again wants nothing to do with me.

I go to the balcony again, and lean against the railing. I need to look around a little, watch the people around me and get my bearings straight.

But rather than regain my composure, I feel the uncertainty of another panic attack coming on. I can hear the surreal question of 'How in the hell did I get here?' being asked over and over in my head. It's louder than the people talking, the people yelling, and the music blasting. It's the only sound I hear. 'How did I get here?' I feel like I've been swimming in an ocean storm, just trying to keep above water, but once I give in to exhaustion, once I've given up, I take one last breath and allow myself the peacefulness of sinking. But I don't die. I find I can hold my breath forever as I drop to the ocean floor. I am beneath everything, swaying like seaweed in the undercurrents, wondering 'How did I get here?' and knowing there is no answer.

Finally I hear a voice next to me, pulling me out. It shouts, "Dude, he's going to puke over the rail!" followed by laughter.

I open my eyes to find myself hunched over the rail, hugging it like a life jacket. I swing my head to the side and can see feet and legs next to me, pointing. Somebody bends over and a face shows up in my view, making a mock vomit sound, and more laughter. I pull myself up, regain my composure as best I can, and turn away. I fight my way to the door outside and into a cab. I need to get back to the hotel. I need to sleep.

That's two panic attacks today. That isn't right.

I finally get back to find the hotel room is freezing cold from the air-conditioning and the bed is empty, still tucked flat from the maids. In the middle of the bed sits the Target Box, waiting patiently in a place I didn't leave it. I look around in my drunken stupor and finally notice Paige, wrapped up in blankets on a cot by the wall. And I know what that means. If things were fine, she'd be in the king-sized bed and there wouldn't be a cot in our room. If she were just mad at me, she might be in the king-sized bed, wrapped up in the covers, and the cot would have been set up for me. But since she was willing to have the cot brought up and willing to sleep in it herself, that means she wants nothing to do with me. At the time, I forget about the stripper, forget that she probably saw me making out with someone else, but I do remember that I can be an asshole now. On this trip I can be an asshole and I don't regret it at all, and that's reason enough for Paige to get her own cot. But why she put the Target Box on the bed, I don't know.

I lie down on top of the covers next to it and look at her for a moment, wondering if she's pretending to be asleep with the lights on and the racket I'm making, but before I can figure it out, I'm asleep myself.

FOLK HERO

Let me repeat, I am not a drunk. There was a time, when I was young and single, when I hung with guys like McCarran, that I could potentially have been called a drunk, at least on weekends. But I eventually matured past that, found other things I wanted to spend my time and effort with, and settled on social drinking, plus a little wine or beer on the weekends with Margaret, but not too much. But I live in Georgia now, and I've never had so much as a hard cider in The Peach State.

But this weekend, well, I'm going to drink as much as I possibly can. Starting yesterday. I'll be worse today. I'll be hung over for days, but I took Monday and Tuesday off, so I can lay in bed and wallow in my near self-immolation. Just like last year. Just like the year before that, and the year before that.

And that's what I'm thinking about, that I'm not a drunk, as I lie beneath the covers with the headache of a drunk. I think I hear the shower, maybe some other noises, as I roll about trying to get comfortable, tucking the covers beneath me, then untucking them, crawling beneath them, then crawling back out.

"Hello?" I finally call out into the room, my scratchy voice sounding hollow in the chilled air.

Paige appears from the bathroom, showered, dressed and finishing her make-up. She bends over next to the bed, picks up the Target Box, and places it on the dresser. "When are you going to finish this?"

"Not today," I say.

"Fine. I'm going out for a while. I'll see you later."

With the drumbeats in my head, I can't help thinking how much I want Paige. How I think she can help me. How I wish she would just spend the day with me. And especially, now that she hates me and wants nothing to do with me, how I can want her without any guilt, how I think I could pledge myself to her completely, as long as she vows not to reciprocate. "Are you heading out?" I ask.

"For a bit."

"Where too?"

"Just out. To get some fresh air."

"When will you get back?"

"I don't know."

I open an eye and look at the clock beside the bed. It's only 9 A.M. "Like an hour?"

"At least two."

"Okay. I'll see you back here at eleven."

She doesn't respond.

"Eleven it is," I say with conviction. "I'll be ready at eleven."

Paige shakes her head as she goes back into the bathroom. I roll around some more until I hear the hallway door open and close without so much as a goodbye.

I can't sleep but I can't get up, so my body and mind just lie there concentrating on the passing seconds, slowly counting minutes. During an acrobatic roll on the bed, I manage to grab the remote and turn on the television. The voices are distracting; they have a comforting distance of coming from somewhere else, until some newscaster on some station mentions the Air and Water Show, and I open my eyes to see a brunette reporting from the North Avenue Bridge with throngs of people passing in the background. Chicago is up and moving, and I'm just lying here. Time to get up. Time to go.

I get up, put on running shorts, a t-shirt and my running shoes, which I packed just in case. My shoes are light and well cushioned, tilting forward so I have to move fast as I head down the hallway, down the elevator and into the lobby. I run three to four times a week, long distances, ranging from ten to twenty miles at a time. No matter how hung-over I am, this consistency has parts of me that are ready to go.

I grab a small Gatorade from the gift-shop, down it in a futile attempt at hydration, then head outside and go east, towards the lake. My legs start slow, my lungs hurting more than they should for such an easy pace.

I run every day because it's something to do. Something healthy to do. Something I'm probably addicted to. I'm at that point where I wake up and just feel like running. Like Forrest Gump.

I love that scene where he says he just felt like running, and once he starts, just keeps going and going until he's crisscrossed America multiple times. It's a purely psychological avoidance issue, an outlet he uses to cope with his life, but it works for him.

Most people can't take their coping mechanisms to such extremes. They starve to death from anorexia, their liver quits after too much drinking, their stomach rips open from too many pills, or most likely, they eventually just grow tired and quit. But Forrest just kept going. No pain. No side-effects. No repercussions. He was kind of a psychological folk hero, a Paul Bunyan of the psychoses. In reality we can't go on forever, we can't be folk heroes, but in reality, 'forever' is overrated. I guess if there's one folk hero we can approach it's John Henry, who gave it his all until there was nothing left to give, then lay down and died, rewarded with a mound of dirt within view of the rail line. If everything goes right, that's the very best we can hope for.

Sometimes I wish I could run forever, leaving everything behind and just have the wind at my back, the pavement under my feet, and the sun on my face. It's especially nice as I meet up with Lake Michigan and head north along the waterfront, my legs finally feeling their groove. If I tried to run forever, my knees would begin to buckle, my back would seize up, and my heart would eventually burst. But it is nice to think about, forgetting the past and just running ahead, step after step forever, running until my heart can't take any more. Of course, when I'm not running, I still feel on pace to having my heart burst.

So I pick up the pace. I do this because it's fun to run fast in Chicago, darting past pedestrians, dog walkers and slow bicyclists. When I run in Athens, there's no need to go fast. The roads are long and open, and the scenery barely changes no matter how fast you go. It's about as exciting as putting a treadmill in the middle of a soy field. But here, I love running fast, and even though I know I'm going to tire myself out, especially after last night, I'll enjoy it while I can.

I hit the lake and head north, running alongside the crowds of people who have gathered for the show. Their necks are bent back as they search the sky, waiting and watching, while I watch them. Finally my breathing gets too hard, my mouth too parched, and I decide to walk a little. Assuming I make it back, I've already run farther than I planned to. I've gone about three miles to Diversey Harbor, and I need to walk a little before heading back.

I'm tired but feeling better, at least physically. The crowds are all waiting, a few talking here and there, and I notice along the pond to my left, the people are watching two little girls, who are taking slow, big steps along the grass, as if they were walking through a minefield. They are sisters, probably both under the age of eight, and they are wearing fancy white dresses, all bows and frills and such, but I'm not sure why others keep looking at them. I watch some more until I hear the boom of an overhead jet, like the skies were wired with explosives and the demolition has just begun. As soon as it hits, the two girls turn and run, screaming the whole way. They run to their dad and hit his legs head on, grabbing on as tight as they can with their eyes pinched shut and their mouths wide open, screaming.

People smile and laugh at the two little girls rather than the aerodynamic marvels hurtling overhead, and the girls know they're putting on a show. It's a funny sight, but it's also comforting, reminding everyone of when the scariest things were things that couldn't hurt us; when holding onto a parent's leg was all we needed for relief. Once the jets have passed, the girls stop screaming and look out to the many faces watching them. They look at each other and then let go, carefully stepping away from their protector, back out into the world, ready to run back at a moment's notice.

I close my eyes, and though I'm walking, it hurts to breathe; my heart is bursting.

I turn around and double time it back to the hotel, distracting myself with speed and pain and the dream of giving it my all until there's nothing to give, like John Henry.

THE END

I was partly responsible too. Not that we ever, ever blamed each other. I can't emphasize that enough. We did not blame each other, not with our words, our actions, our heads or our hearts. We knew the weight of blame and could never do that to each other. We knew the weight because we blamed ourselves and knew the burden was too high to place on someone else's shoulders, too all-encompassing to think someone could actually be the cause of such perpetuity, that someone could strip away the world we lived in to reveal the one we now inhabit.

My part was just a small comment, and though it had ramifications, I uttered it as innocuously as I would comment about the color of a belt. It was almost a joke. But I can't say it was insignificant, as everything was significant that day.

We had just moved from the city to the western suburbs, Naperville, and bought a house. Margaret built a studio in the basement, and her photography business couldn't have been doing better. I took a train into the city, to Rush Hospital where I worked. We had a yard with a swing set, a garage with Evelyn's Big Wheel and training bike. We had all sorts of suburban amenities, and everything in the house seemed big compared to our place in the city. The schools were new, and like-minded parents were moving in around us. This was the place where we would raise our daughter. This would be her home.

Amongst those amenities was an upstairs laundry. It wasn't big, a hallway snuggled between the master bedroom and the upstairs bathroom, but it was a lot bigger than the units stacked in a closet in our old condo. The previous owners insisted on taking their units for some reason, so we had a new washer and dryer installed right after moving in. That night Margaret called for me from upstairs. I put Evelyn in the pack-and-play and went upstairs to see what she needed.

"This machine doesn't work," Margaret said, leaning over the washing machine and pushing buttons.

"What?"

"It won't turn on."

"I saw it on this afternoon," I said, having been home when it was installed while Margaret was doing a photoshoot at the River Walk. "They had the water running and the spinner going."

"Well it won't even turn on now."

I stood next to her and pushed the big button labeled Power.

"I tried that," she said.

"I know you did," I sighed, "but I'm going to try it too. Does the dryer turn on?"

"I don't know."

I reached out and pressed its Power button. "They're both out," I said, "that doesn't make sense. Must be something with the electricals."

"The electricals?" Margaret asked.

We now owned a house, and I knew this would not be the last time I felt a fool for not being handy. "The electricity. The wiring. The circuit breaker. Let me look in the back." I grabbed the edges of the washing machine and pulled, but it wasn't budging. I then moved over to the dryer, and with a see-sawing push-pull I managed to move it a few inches from the wall. I leaned over the side and peered at the cables and wiring behind. I saw two plugs in their socket, and beyond that had no idea what I was looking at. I was curious why the dryer stopped moving, and staring at the hoses for a while, saw that the gas line had been pulled tight as it started at the bottom of the dryer next to me, but went to the opposite side behind the washer, up high. There wasn't much give. "That's not good," I said to myself.

"What's not good?"

"Oh, nothing. It's the gas line. It barely reaches from the wall over there to the dryer."

"What does that mean?"

"Nothing. I don't think. I'll push the dryer back in and it'll be fine." And then I said it, "It's just that if the dryer starts moving, like with an uneven load, it'll pull on the gas line." I was just talking out loud, not realizing what I said, what it would mean to Margaret.

"And then what?"

"Nothing. You just don't want the gas line getting pulled out or anything. You don't mess around with gas."

"What'll happen?"

"I'm sure it's fine. Don't worry about it. Everything looks plugged in back here, but could you get me a flashlight?"

"Sure."

Margaret started to leave and flipped the two switches by the doorway. The overhead light went off but the washer and dryer sprung to life, with a beep and sweep of flashing lights. "Shit," I said, "they put them on a switch. Why the hell would they do that?"

And that was that. I once went to Home Depot to see if they had a longer gas line, but they didn't. I wasn't going to hire someone for something as straightforward as replacing a hose that was working fine, and I wasn't going to complain to the department store that installed it. I'm sure they used the longest one in the kit. In retrospect, I'm not sure how much of this reasoning was before and how much was after, as I don't remember thinking much about it at all.

But I do remember a few weeks later, I think it was a Saturday, making lunch in the kitchen. Evie was packing plastic fruit into the plastic refrigerator of her plastic kitchen, when that deep thudding sound began emanating from the ceiling. I barely looked up, barely had time to ask what that was, when I heard water running, a flush from the upstairs bedroom, followed by footsteps racing into the laundry room. I smiled and pushed down on the Panini press, realizing Margaret had stopped the unbalanced load in under ten seconds, and that she had to go back to the bathroom to wash her hands. I realized Margaret was concerned about the gas line, but didn't really connect the dots, that she was afraid her house was going to blow up. She was trying to save us all. I looked up and watched Evie put a plastic orange into her plastic microwave and completely forgot about the gas line.

It was Saturday, June 22nd. There were two grocery stores, a Dominick's and a Jewel, equidistant from our house. Margaret said Jewel had better produce, but they also always seemed to have long lines. Dominick's produce was good enough for the shrimp tacos I planned to make that night, and they had a Starbucks inside the store, so I went to Dominick's. I loved shrimp tacos, still do, which I'm slightly surprised about. I will still eat them, but I won't ever make them again.

I remember the grocery list because I hated going to the store for so few items:

Shrimp
Cabbage
Cilantro
White Onion
Chips
Roma Tomatoes
Eggs
Milk
Coffee Filters

We already had chipotle peppers, but I grabbed another can. I didn't get tortillas because I had corn flour and would make my own. Margaret got me a tortilla press for my birthday the year before and they were kind of a pain to make and not any better than the store bought ones, but there's more authenticity when homemade. The tomatoes were meant for chips and salsa. The cilantro would be used in both. I picked up some single-serve yogurt, the Light and Fit kind, and walked to the lady standing at a table offering samples at the end of the wine aisle. I smiled and said no thank-you, just curious what she had but not really wanting anything. Beer was the best match for a shrimp taco, and I walked down the cooler aisle to grab something. Miller Lite was $11.99 for a sixteen pack of cans while bottles of Dos Equis had a red sign under their price signifying a good deal, $10.99 for a twelve pack. I knew Dos Equis was more expensive than Miller, so it wasn't a direct comparison, but I stood there thinking unaware as time roiled on, hands grasping the grocery cart handle, and thought about what to get. I have no idea what calculations I did; it wasn't rational because I can tell you now that I was going to get the Dos Equis regardless of price, and maybe I was justifying it to myself. Why I got the twelve pack of imported beer doesn't matter, but I did stand there, eyes darting back and forth, thinking the passing time didn't matter. But it did matter. It mattered so fucking much.

I had less than twelve items, was third in line in the fifteen-items-or-less checkout, avoiding getting stuck behind the overflowing carts carrying a week's worth of groceries. The first lady might have had more than fifteen items, but the checkout lady swiped the soup cans so quickly it didn't matter. The guy in front of me had flowers and a card and looked anxious. I read the magazines as the bagboy went off to get a plastic sleeve for the bouquet, but the man was already checked out and waiting as the cashier began swiping my items. Older, with thin glasses and 'Dorothy' printed on her nametag, she was all business. Working quickly, she identified cilantro without having to read the band holding them together, typed in the codes for onions, tomatoes and cabbage from memory, and had me checked out and bagged before the bagboy had returned with a sleeve for the man's flowers. She wouldn't let any customer's small talk distract her from the mission at hand. If I needed to get out of there quickly, Dorothy was the one to do it. If I needed to get out of there quickly, I couldn't blame Dorothy. I signed my name with the plastic pen, nodded as she handed me the receipt, grabbed my plastic bags and left.

I didn't stop to support the high school band, walking past the teenagers peddling candy bars. Even the lights worked in my favor. I had a red on Maple, but was turning right and the turn lane was wide open. "Smooth" was playing on the radio, one of those perfect summer songs that came out a few years earlier, I think when Evelyn was born. I tapped my fingers on the steering wheel, opened the sun roof and sang along to lyrics I didn't know. It was hot and playful, and the only thing I had to do when I got home was crack open a Dos Equis, cook dinner and relax. We would eat outside, I thought. It was a little hot, a little sticky, and the sunset was

84

usually pretty blinding in our treeless backyard, but a little music from the radio could entice you to hold Evelyn's hands and dance.

Evelyn.

I backed the Taurus into the garage and with one hand grabbed the two plastic bags off the passenger side floor, the gallon of milk with the other. "Man it's a hot one…" I mouthed to myself, repeating the first lyric over and over. Once out, I put the side of my leg against the door and pushed it shut. I walked six steps, climbed the two steps into the house, and opened the door with the hand holding the milk. Inside, swallowed by air-conditioning, I pushed the door shut with my ass and kicked my Birkenstocks into the closet.

I heard the voice from above, shouting but nonchalant, drifting down the stairs. "Can you check on Evie? I'll be right down."

I walked into the kitchen, saw the plate, and immediately knew what happened, envisioned every step and action like I was in the room when it happened. Margaret had been making lunch for Evelyn, a patch of corn niblets still nestled in the groove on Evelyn's Elmo plate. Margaret must have been slicing the hot dog when it started. Margaret held the hot dog on one end, put the knife in by her fingers and sliced the length of the hot dog. She then gave it a quarter turn and repeated, making four long strands of hot dog protruding from her left hand. She then started at the right side and began chopping, making four quarters of a coin with every slice, tiny little meat triangles for Evie to spread around on her plate, throw on the floor, and eventually eat. While chopping, the washer's bang-bang-bang from an unbalanced load began pounding through the ceiling. She must have quickly finished chopping down the hot dog and threw it onto the plate, dropping it in front of Evelyn as she ran upstairs, forgetting that the end she held onto, less than an inch used for grip, had never been quartered and was a big 'ole chunk that needed to be chewed. One fucking piece.

When I think of dropped groceries, I think of eggs, their delicate shells cracking, their unborn contents slopping out in a sticky run of yellow across a translucent goo. But the eggs, brown organic eggs encased in a plastic see-through container, landed without incident. As the two plastic grocery bags landed, it was the roma tomatoes that seemed to hit the hardest. Eight of them, bouncing against each other inside their own clear produce bag, bouncing against each other before setting one free, which rolled out from the bags, across the kitchen tiles. I didn't care about that tomato, I could make salsa with just seven, but somewhere in my head I thought, *The tomatoes are bruised.*

That's what I thought. It wasn't important. It was so, so, so, so fucking unimportant, but that thought flashed. And after releasing the grocery bags, as I ran toward the far end of the table, I placed the milk gallon on the table. It took half a second, at most. It didn't matter, but why would I do that? Why not just drop the milk too?

I lost my sense of sound first. I couldn't hear a thing as I screamed, "Call 9-1-1!" Like noise vibrations on the ocean floor, I could not hear or process my own screams. I lost the sense of touch next. My knees buckled and I jammed my side against the table edge as I lifted Evie out of her high chair. There was a flash of hot dog smell, that moist, acrid rubber, cold and processed, but then it was gone. I could not smell anymore. I think I tasted Evelyn as I placed my mouth against hers, but it was a foreign, lost taste, already gone. And as I breathed, as I pumped, as I breathed, as I pumped, as I breathed, as I pumped, I lost my sight. Evelyn was gone, choked on an unsliced-morsel-of-processed-pig-stuffed-intestine gone. As I breathed, as I pumped, as I breathed, as I pumped, as I breathed, as I pumped…

As I breathed, Evelyn did not.

REHYDRATE. DEHYDRATE.

RINSE. REPEAT.

I walk the last block to the hotel, allowing my heartbeat to begin recovering while a slight breeze cools the sweat from my body. Upon entering the lavish lobby I head towards the hotel bar. A few people sit at round tables in horseshoe chairs, sipping their beer and watching baseball on the TVs tucked in the upper corners. I survey the bottles of hard alcohol and order a Gatorade and a shot of vodka.

"You just go running?" asks the bartender, straightening his bow tie.

"Yep. Nice day out there."

He sets both drinks in front of me and I down the purple one first. The Yankees are beating the Red Sox and I watch without much surprise or care. I put the shot in my mouth and let it swirl, let the burning vapors of alcohol settle, and then swallow. I doubt the bartender gets many orders like that. A Gatorade and a shot. A rehydrator and a dehydrator. Binge and purge. Living at odds with oneself. Conflict. Extremes. "And now," I tell the bartender, "it's breakfast time. How about a Bloody Mary?"

He pauses with a questioning, concerned look. "You sure, buddy?"

"Positive," surprised I got called buddy on my second drink. It's a Saturday morning, but I imagine he can tell who's having two for the day and who's just getting started. I love when the bartender calls you buddy. There's nothing sadder than when the man who serves alcohol for a living tries to befriend you in hopes that you'll stop drinking. I wonder if that ever works? I wonder if an alcoholic, which I've already explained that I'm not, ever listens to this friendly advice. If the alcoholic thinks, hey, that guy just called me buddy and said I should probably stop drinking, so hey, I'll stop this train-without-brakes that's ruining my life for him. I haven't stopped drinking for my wife, my kids, my job, anyone or anything, but I'll do it for the guy behind the bar. Thanks for caring, Buddy.

I take my drink and go upstairs. By the time I hit the shower, I can feel the draining effects of my run filling in with booze. Once I've cleaned up and put on something new, I feel good, cracking a light beer out of the mini-fridge and propping myself on the newly made bed, watching the local coverage of the air show on TV and waiting for Paige.

She eventually comes in empty-handed and neither of us asks where the other has been.

"A beer?" she asks, "Already?"

"Gotta ride that shampoo effect," I say.

"The what?"

"Shampoo effect."

"What's that?"

"You know how after you shampoo your hair, lather it up and wash it out, how you can take just the smallest dab of shampoo, put it in, and your hair will completely lather up again?"

"Yeah."

"Well after a hard night drinking, you can have a single beer the next morning and be right back to where you started. The shampoo effect." And that's just one beer. I'm not sure what the technical term is for a hard run, a shot of vodka, a Bloody Mary and then a beer.

"Fascinating."

"I thought so too. So, what do you want to do today?" I ask.

"I see that's still here," Paige says, pointing to the Target Box beside the TV. She sits down on a chair in the corner and rests her elbow on her knees, her chin in her hands.

"Yep. Here until tomorrow."

"Let's talk about last night," she says, and I so wish I hadn't just turned off the TV.

"All right. Let's discuss last night."

"I saw you."

"You saw me?"

"Yes, at that dance club. Kissing that girl in yellow."

I think for a moment. This could put a serious damper on the weekend. I'm half- tempted to go with denial, like the guy whose wife comes home and finds him in bed with another woman. He keeps denying and denying, even as his mistress gets dressed and leaves. He just denies she was ever in the room. By the end, his wife gives up and asks him what he wants for dinner. I don't think that will work here, but I understand the concept; don't make a big deal out of it. "And now you don't trust me."

"Of course not."

"Good."

"Good?"

"Good." And I wait for a moment, letting her anger at me being a smug asshole turn into wonder, wondering how I can be smug about being such an asshole. "Listen Paige, I can be as nice as possible, but it's important that you know not to trust me. I can be kind and considerate most of the time, and if we're friends, then there's nothing to worry about. But there are times when, well, if we try to become anything more than friends, it's better if you just don't trust me too much."

Paige just looks at me wondering what the hell? Nobody ever says they can't be trusted, at least this blatantly. And I am mad at myself for being this honest, but I'm not mad at myself for being this way, because for one weekend I just don't give a fuck.

"So what are you, a serial cheater?"

"No, not at all. Nothing like that at all. Let's just say I have certain problems with relationships, serious relationships, boy-girl relationships." I point to her and me as I say boy-girl, as if she doesn't know who's who. I don't know why. "I just don't have relationships."

"That's sad."

"Probably. If you're outside looking in, I'm sure it looks that way. But it's not as sad as what can happen if I did have a relationship. What does happen."

"But...," Paige starts, ready to defend relationships with the ending of every Rom-Com she's ever seen, every romance novel she's ever read, and every happily-ever-after ending she's ever dreamed. But I give her a look that says this weekend is not the start of a Rom-Com, and I am not a happily-ever-after. "So what are we supposed to do?" she asks.

"About this whole thing?" And now I circle my hand in the air, as if she doesn't know what this whole thing is.

"Yes."

"Nothing. Let's have fun like we did yesterday. More fun. I was thinking we could take the El up to Wrigley Field. The game starts in about an hour."

She eyes me wearily.

"I promise you'll have a good time," I say. And I mean it. "That's how you can trust me. You'll have fun. We'll have fun. Expectations of nothing more and nothing less and we're good. Okay?"

Paige leans back and pulls her legs into the chair with her, unsure of even the safety of the floor. "But why are you...?"

"I just am."

"Fine." She mulls it over and I sip my beer, trying to drink at an awkward angle as I lay there, making a slurping sound to fill the void. When it all clicks for her, she gets up and goes to her bag, unzips it and starts digging inside.

I wonder if she's so mad she's going to leave. And she should be mad, because I should have told her not to trust me before inviting her to Chicago for the weekend, before holding her hand in the art museum and dancing with her at the nightclub. I should have told her before we kissed on the dance club floor and before she confided that she really liked me. But that's not the way relationships work. You need to get down in the shit before you know what's going on.

I also wonder how mad she would be if she knew what thoughts were going through my head. That watching her bend over her luggage, hair falling at her sides as her legs hold erect and her torso bends against her tight shorts, I can't help think how much I want her. The fact that I now can't have her, have told her not to open her heart to me and had her agree to it, makes me want to grab her from behind, hold her tight, and kiss the back of her neck until she squirms around and kisses me back or beats the hell out of me. I wonder how mad she would be if she knew I was already planning on flirting with her even more today? I wonder how mad she will be the first time I try to hold her hand? Or the first time I try to kiss her?

Of course, there is the possibility that she'll be more interested in me. Eventually. Once she realizes she can't have me, or shouldn't, that I've got trouble written all over me, I wonder if she'll want me even more. There are so many women and men that want what they can't have; I can't help but feel hopeful.

I don't have time to dwell on it too long, because Paige finds what she's looking for, pulls it out and holds it against her chest, a St. Louis Cardinals jersey. "I believe the Cards are in town today."

"Hot damn," I say, forgetting people from southern Illinois were traitorous baseball snakes. I'm not going to say anything, but now I know I can't trust her either. We're even. "Looks like a great day for some baseball."

LOVABLE LOSERS

Paige and I catch the Red Line north, hoping we can get to Wrigley Field and scalp tickets before the game starts. If we don't, we can always just watch it at the surrounding bars. The experience of a Cubs game is not restricted to just being inside the ballpark, although it's the best way to go. The neighborhood is the experience. The excitement starts hours before game time and will continue into the morning when bars along Clark and Sheffield, the North-South streets on each side of Wrigley Field, finally close.

People in blue and red are all around us, showing their support for the Cubs-Cards rivalry. As we wedge our way into some sort of line near the scalpers, I hear two kids behind us, about the same age as when I lived in Chicago and went to games, begin their catchy, ever-inspiring cheer, "St. Louis Sucks! St. Louis Sucks!"

Paige ignores the first rally cry, the second and the third. But the fourth time they start cheering she turns and looks at them, two kids in their mid-twenties, both wearing Cubs t-shirts, one with a Cubs floppy hat and the other wearing blue and red beads around his neck. "Are you kidding me?" she asks. "Do you want me to compare St. Louis to the Cubs? Take your pick: pitching, hitting, or fielding? St. Louis has you beat in every category. The only stat I can think we'd lose is most home runs by a player named Sammy. Of course that goes along with most strikeouts. Or did you mean historically the Cubs are better? I know I don't even have to mention their last World Series? When was the last time they won the division? Made the playoffs? It's August and who's completely out of contention? Not the Cardinals. If St. Louis sucks, the Cubs are the pieces of shit that should have been flushed a long time ago, and that goes double for you two shithead fans who don't seem to know any better."

The two kids look at each other in shock, not expecting more than a dirty look from Paige, maybe a stern, "Fuck off," which would have only made them laugh. They never meant to get into details. They're Cubs fans, lovable losers, who produce high hopes that fall apart by the All Star game, year after year, until nobody cares or expects anything more. But at least they're putting their hopes into something that doesn't matter. I mean, the worst that could possibly happen is the Cubs go 0-163. That's it. And even if that happened, by mid-season, they'd probably be a phenomenon for being so bad, like the phenomenon of not winning a world series for approaching a hundred years. So there's no downside, since nobody expects anything in the first place. The games are fun, the fans are fun, the bleachers and vendors and streets full of people are fun. And that's enough for me.

There's always one come-back that I lead with. Cub-haters argue that Cubs fans are not true baseball fans, especially the bleacher bums. They sit in the hot sun, drink, and socialize with the people around them, yelling occasionally, watching a little of the game but mainly keeping an eye on their cup game or mound ball betting. They leave after the sixth inning regardless of the score. Afterwards they don't remember who pitched, but they do have a vague idea if Sosa hit a homerun and whether or not the Cubs were winning when they left. So when chastised for not being a true baseball fan, my response was a simple, "Yes." Absolutely. You're not going to catch me studying the line-up, keeping score, or debating when the closer should come in. It's a party, and we're here to party, no matter what the players do on the field.

Once Paige has finished chastising the two boys behind me, who are still waiting behind us with heads down, I turn to Paige's ear and quietly chant, "St. Louis Sucks. St. Louis Sucks." The two boys join in for another round and we high-five each other, while Paige gives me the evil eye.

We manage to get bleacher tickets, although at an exorbitant price. Bleacher seats used to be ten dollars, but whatever. Inside we get two beers and two pretzels, the latter at my suggestion. (I don't explicitly tell Paige not to get a hot dog, but I also don't ask.) We sit in deep center field, beyond the ivy, beneath the last manual scoreboard in baseball, and try to watch the game. People talk and cheer around us, filled in by the occasional blast of music between innings. Twice a group of jet planes makes their way this far north from the air show and fly by low and loud. The excited sounds of activity are all around us, and I feel alive.

I look around but nobody seems to be playing any games, so I turn to the two couples sitting behind us who seem to be together and ask if they want to play the cup game. They ask the rules and I explain. Everyone puts a dollar in the cup and one person starts off holding the cup, which gets passed around between batters. When you have the cup, you have whomever is up to bat. If they get an out, you put another dollar in. A single, you take a dollar out. A double you take two, and a triple three. If your batter hits a home run you get all the money in the cup, everyone puts in another buck and we start over. Nice and simple. Game on.

There are five home-runs during the game, and Paige manages to have the cup for two while I have it for one (a Sammy Sosa home run, which I argue should pay double). We also manage to get a few doubles as well as quite a few walks, which equates to us taking about twenty bucks from the couples behind us, who seem confused and eventually annoyed every time I tell them they owe another buck. They aren't happy about losing, and they especially aren't happy that I keep laughing when they lose, standing up to do a little gloating dance every time Paige or I take more of their money. But they are nice couples, and when the Cardinals are crushing the Cubs 9-2 in the seventh inning stretch, they tell us to keep the money in the cup because they're leaving for a drink at Murphy's bleachers.

Half the people in the bleachers have gone by the eighth inning when the Cubs score two runs and are still down 9-4. Paige says there's no way she's leaving the game early, and I don't argue.

"Na na na, na," I belt out, and then look at Paige expectantly.

After a moment she meekly replies, "Na na na, na."

And then we both finish, her softly beneath my exuberant shouts, "Hey hey hey, good-bye."

I repeat this throughout the ninth as Paige sings her part with more fervor. We sing it after the Cubs get runners on second and third. We sing it after they get a two-run double and close within three runs. We sing it after the batter pops a single over the second basemen's head and runners are at the corners with one out and the tying run is at the plate. And when he hits a game-tying homerun into the left field bleachers, we jump up and high-five everyone around us, confirming we were right not to leave, not to give up.

There's a quick strike out at the plate, ending the inning, and so we sing as the players change sides. This time I coordinate the fans I was just giving high-fives to on my left to sing the first line of na-nas, while those on my right sing the next line, and we all finish together.

Na na na, na. Na na na, na. Hey hey hey, good-bye.

Na na na, na. Na na na, na. Hey hey hey, good-bye.

And even though Paige was cheering on the Cardinals, she is also cheering the lowly Cubs, whose ass the sun seems to be shining on today. And we all sing along as the Cardinals get runners on first and second, but a double play sends us to the bottom of the tenth, everything tied.

Na na na, na. Na na na, na. Hey hey hey, good-bye.

Na na na, na. Na na na, na. Hey hey hey, good-bye.

The chant is now beyond my control; if anyone starts it everyone joins in. To others around, if there's anyone sober, it's probably really annoying, but it's our chant, our cheer, and we're all cheering together. The Cub's record doesn't matter, that their season is statistically over doesn't matter. The lovable losers are going to pull off a come-from-behind upset, we all believe it and we couldn't ask for more.

Na na na, na. Na na na, na. Hey hey hey, good-bye.

We sing as the first Cubs batter gets a single, a sacrifice bunt advances him to second, a right field pop-up advances him to third, and a broken bat sends the ball between first and second, sending our runner home. Cubs win! Cubs win! We all dance and cheer and high-five and hug one another. This is the apex of my drunkenness, of my joy. I'll remember this game as a montage of jokes and laughs, gambling with strangers, the Cubs winning and everyone claiming they're having the best time ever. This should be the moment to ride the rest of the night on, a full tank of joy that will propel us through midnight. As we work our way out, everyone heading towards the exits en masse, I hear our chant repeated from various groups along the walkway.

Na na na, na. Na na na, na. Hey hey hey, good-bye.

We make our way outside, merging into the crowds shuffling away from the stadium and into a beautiful afternoon full of promise. Paige doesn't seem to mind when I take her hand, making sure we don't get separated among the crisscrossing crowds along Addison, then compress into a bunch before the police wave a large group across Clark. When things open up a bit, Paige doesn't seem to mind that I don't let go. We decide to eat something more than beers and pretzels, and enter a bar down Clark Street called John Barleycorn. It's a nice bar for this area, bedecked with wood floors and wood paneling. Old art paintings line the walls, and the back wall has a display of model wooden ships. Most of the tables are taken, and a number of people have congregated around the bar, but the hostess manages to get us a table for two.

STUPID PEOPLE

Paige and I talk about the game, and she goes into her love of baseball, a sport her dad idolized, watching whenever he could, the Cardinals being his one true source of pleasure over the years. And as such, his only child, his little girl, learned to sit on the couch next to him and cheer the little players on the television when he did, belittle the opposing team when he did, criticize the announcer for inane comments when he did, and follow the constant diatribes about what or who was ruining baseball today, followed by what had once made it great. And listening to her talk excitedly, I could sense not only her love of the game, but also her love of being daddy's little girl.

And I can't help once again finding Paige attractive. She's an independent woman who doesn't seem to trust the world too much. And I'm sure I haven't helped that situation. But she's confident in herself, poignant in her comments as she dabs her fries in ketchup and eats them, licking her lips and curiously looking about her. Her Cardinals jersey is unbuttoned, and once again I can study the long, sexy tendons pulling from her sun-reddened chest to her neck. Her silver-ringed fingers glide over her food and pick at her napkin, holding everything between the pads of her fingers, maintaining her distance.

"You know, you're a smart girl," I tell her out of the blue. Flattery always works, but flattery where they don't expect it, where they want to be flattered, that always works best. We all want to believe we're special.

"How so?" she asks cautiously.

"Well, I mean I don't know if you're good at astrophysics or anything..."

"I'm not."

"But you know what's going on around you."

"Maybe," she says, but not ready to trust me. "I bet you think you're pretty smart too."

"I used to. I definitely used to, but I don't know anymore. More likely, I'm pretty stupid, just..."

"Just what?"

"It's just that there are a lot of people even stupider than me."

"Stupider?"

95

"Exactly," I say, "stupider."

"That is true."

"Which part? That I'm pretty stupid?"

Paige holds up a fry and points it at me. "Probably, but that's not what I meant." She curiously looks at the fry, wondering why it's being used as a pointer, and puts it into her mouth. "I just agree there are a lot of stupid people out there."

"Most definitely."

"But," she continues, "that's not an excuse. If I've learned anything, I've learned that. The stupid people may rule the world, but if you use that as an excuse, it's your own fault for whatever happens to you."

"Really?"

"You want to know why I quit cheerleading?"

"Yes," I say. And we're no longer in a crowded bar talking about baseball. We are now at home on the couch, discussing life over a bottle of wine. We're two patients on the psych couch, telling our problems to each other. We're at confession.

"It's no big surprise. I got pregnant when I was a junior. And everyone told me it would ruin my life, that I should get an abortion. But I didn't, I couldn't, and I had a beautiful baby girl that next year. I never even told the father, even though he was the only man I had been with. He was too afraid to ask. I'm sure he knew he was the father but never wanted to know, which was fine because I didn't want him in my life anymore. So with my mother's help, I was determined to raise my little girl all by myself."

"What about your dad?" I asked.

"He had a heart attack two years before. Had one while out on his tractor, in the middle of his cornfield. The tractor just sat there idling while he passed away."

"I'm sorry."

"Thanks," Paige said, and paused because she was supposed to. "So I finished high school, got an apartment down the street from my mother, and raised my girl on my own."

"That had to be tough."

"That's exactly what all the stupid people said."

"Thanks again."

"Sorry. But people told me I should be happy I was getting by, happy with my crummy job and my crummy apartment because I was a single mom. They told me it was normal to go out on dates but never get a boyfriend because guys didn't want a ready-made family. The one smart thing people told me was I should give everything I had to my baby girl, but they also implied that I should have nothing left for myself. And so I gave her everything, did my very best with her, and never tried to have anything for myself."

I look at my food getting cold, knowing I can't eat until she's done. So I sip my beer and listen, wondering what it would be like to listen to Paige talk in bed, the late night talking where her head lies on your arm and her hair presses the side of your face, both of you talking to the ceiling about the world's troubles.

"Whenever I went on a date, I would tell him right away, 'You're not going to like me.' I'd tell him that I had a daughter, and that it would be all right if he never called me back, that I understood. I let him off the hook, because all the stupid people told me he wouldn't call me anyway. But I should have said, 'I'm a single mother and I'm one hell of a catch.' That's what I should have said."

"And you would have been right," I said, although Paige didn't care about my opinion. She knew she was right.

"For work I took the first job I could get. I should be glad anyone would hire a single mother with a high school diploma. That's what all the stupid people told me. So I did. I went to work every day, thinking I was lucky to slave for everyone else who made the real money and the real decisions, just glad to have a job, no matter how hard or how well I performed. Meanwhile I kept my mouth shut as they hired new people ahead of me, people who were lazy, incompetent, and sometimes just plain stupid. I would show them how to do everything, fix the mistakes they made, and then watch them get promoted while I was glad to get a long lunch so I could take my daughter to the dentist."

I can't say anything. I pull my knee up to my chest and hug it, still leaning forward and letting her know I'm interested. I'm fascinated.

"That's the problem with listening to all the stupid people. You begin to think the same way they do; you become just as stupid as they are."

"That's probably true."

"My baby girl got a scholarship to the University of Illinois. Between that and the money I've saved up, she's going to have all four years paid for. She left last week and is trying out for their cheerleading squad. And for the first time in eighteen years, I'm home alone."

"Are you ready for that?"

"I'm going to be fine. More than fine. I talk to her every day, and just like she's starting her new life, so am I. I'm thirty-five years old. I told my boss that if I didn't get a promotion, a well-deserved promotion, I was leaving. And I got it. I'm also signed up for night classes at the junior college, which he's paying for. It may be late, but I'm starting over again."

"That's fantastic," I say. And I envy Paige. She has a mantra for her life, her goals laid out before her, and a strong sense that things are important. I almost hope everything works out for her. Almost. But then I remember where I am, why I am, and that she's just telling her sentimental claptrap story of how she wants the world to work. The people who told her to be satisfied were stupid, but she's just as stupid to think she shouldn't be, that she deserves more. We're all stupid because we're all wrong, I'm certain of that. We are all wrong, always, and we become stupid the moment we forget that.

"I'm excited, but I should have done this twenty years ago."

I'm suddenly worried what I'll say next, so it's time to change the subject. "What's her name?"

And Paige pauses. She's brought back from her declaration, her vow of transformation, brought back to something she loves. Someone she loves. And I know I've asked the right question. "Julie," she says, reaching over and squeezing my hand and releasing. "Her name is Julie."

GEARS AND COGS

I think like a psychologist which, like all coins, has two sides. After going to school and learning different theories about what motivates people, the technical terms and theories for what makes them happy and what makes them sad, and then after all the years of people sitting in my office and discussing their problems, I now always look for the reasons behind people's actions. There's always something else to blame for people who are rude, mean-spirited, impatient, annoying, or whatever. This can lead to a forgiving spirit, but the same is true for people who are kind, generous and compassionate, you have to forgive them too.

So after a while I sometimes think of people as machines. I don't know what the gears behind everyone are aligned to do, how they got put together, but I do know they exist, behind the facade. It's the difference between a child at a magic show, one who actually believes in magic and their mystical powers from beyond explanation, and the cynical adult, who may not know how a trick is done, but always, always knows it's nothing more than optical illusions mixed with slight-of-hand.

And because I need to analyze people's feelings, it becomes difficult to show my own. I find myself sitting back and watching more than I should, seldom getting caught up in the social interactions that take place around me. There's always a show going on, and though I may be in the front row, I'm only there to watch.

Margaret used to call me out on that. "You're not working," was the nice way she said it. "Cut the psycho-analysis bullshit," was the not-so-nice way. But either way, I usually needed it. Margaret made sure I stayed human.

As I said, there are two sides to every coin. I may not let my own emotions out, preferring to watch and critique everyone else, but I'm not one of those fools who is led by every emotion he has, sucked into the vacuum of impulses and urges without ever understanding why they exist or how to overcome them when they're wrong. I used to wonder which side was better, but have come to the conclusion: heads, you lose; tails, you still lose.

HARD TOP

I went for a long run that morning, through a light on-and-off drizzle that would leave the rest of the day overcast and wet. It was late September, cool but comfortable, but with that permeating sense of permanent cold coming any day. Margaret was out all morning. She didn't tell me where she was going. I didn't ask and I never wondered when she would return. It had only been four months since the incident, and things weren't getting better. Before the incident I didn't watch much baseball and spent most of my spare time watching Evie. Now I was worried how I would distract myself once the season was over. I desperately needed something to distract me, and the Bears only played one game a week. But for now I had baseball, and was trying to root for other teams so I could enjoy postseason baseball, which would get me through a few more weeks. I was lying on the couch, knees wrapped in ice, watching the Red Sox play Baltimore.

"I've got a surprise," Margaret said from the kitchen, as if she'd been there all morning.

"What?"

"Come outside and see."

For a moment I was curious. I was distracted wondering about a surprise, but only for a moment as thoughts returned to Evelyn. My stomach clenched as I swallowed away the acid returning to my throat, wondering how anything could be labeled a surprise after the surprise of finding your daughter slumped over blue in her high chair. I didn't expect Margaret to really have a surprise, something that I would have never guessed in a million years, one that would keep me distracted for the rest of the day. Really, actually distracted. Distracted enough to keep the haunting memories at bay, and for an afternoon remain unaware of the massive hole in our lives.

I saw it parked on the street and my first thought was that it couldn't be the surprise; someone else must have parked a red Mustang hard-top in front of our house, and instead I looked around for some other surprise. Margaret walked across our suburban lawn, right up to the passenger door, and as she reached out I still kept thinking the surprise must be something else, up until she opened the door and asked, "Would you like to join me for a ride?"

My brow twisted and my eyes squinted, studying Margaret, until she said, "I don't know. I just saw it in the paper and I wanted it." And that was that.

I first wondered how she could want anything, really actually want something enough to go out and get it. I got hungry and ate. I showered. I slept and I woke. I went to work. But I didn't really want to do these things. They were habits, routines, and to stop doing them would only be because I wanted to stop doing them. I really couldn't imagine wanting anything ever again, besides the impossible. So how could Margaret want something?

But as a psychologist, I knew this was good. This was a step, and at this point a step is huge progress. I wasn't ready for progress but I was happy that Margaret was. I really was happy for her. I didn't care how much it cost. I wouldn't have cared if her surprise was that she wanted to join the circus and there was a trapeze set up in the backyard, or if there were a pack of Huskies ready to train for Iditarod. She wanted something, anything, so good for her.

"You remember I had one of these when I was a kid," she said as I got in. I tried to remember while she walked around to the driver's side and got in. I didn't even know she could drive stick. "It's the same year, I think. '84. My dad must have been having a mid-life crisis, since he sold it a year later, but I'd just turned sixteen and to a certain degree thought it was mine. It was the best car I ever had. This one is the same year, the same color, but it's a hard top instead of a convertible."

"I think you mentioned it, but I don't think I actually believed you. Your dad cruising around in a red convertible? I can't even imagine it."

"He didn't even use it that much, he just washed it a lot."

"Now that I can picture. Old Jerry listening to Prince while washing his Little Red Corvette."

"It's a Mustang," Margaret corrected me.

"I know. It's just the song..." I start, but Margaret revs the engine, the first time louder than any engine had ever been revved in our neighborhood, then a second time twice as loud, where the rumble felt like the engine was about to blow through the hood.

"Feel that?" she asked.

"Feel what?" I confirmed.

She didn't peel out or anything, but firmly took us down Oxbow and on to Archer, which was wide open and had a speed limit of fifty. She slowly accelerated, coming to terms with the power of her new toy. "That summer, we were the coolest girls ever, just driving around town with the top down, doing our best to be seen everywhere while pretending we had somewhere to go, singing along to our Greatest Hits tapes as loud as we could."

"What did you listen to?"

"Madonna, of course. Prince. I remember really getting into an OMD tape. I just thought it had the perfect summer songs."

"OMD? You're kidding me. Orchestral Maneuvers in the Dark?"

"And what great music were you listening to in high school?"

"Sixteen? Junior year? I was probably just getting out of my Classic Rock phase and moving on to Iron Maiden."

"And you're giving me shit? You probably had all those stupid Eddie posters hanging on your walls?"

That's so Margaret. I don't know how she even knows the name of the Iron Maiden mascot, a zombie-like creature who adorned all their covers. And how would she know I'd be the type of kid to hang them over my bed? Margaret could be so annoying. "How do you know about Eddie?" I ask her.

"I just know things."

"You do, do you?"

"I do."

This has been a running joke between us since we met. And to be perfectly honest, it's true. Margaret seems to just know things that she shouldn't. Whether it be pop culture, world history, economic theory, wine tasting, or whatever, she seems to know something about every topic. She wasn't a know-it-all either; she just pulled out these little facts when appropriate. I could now add heavy-metal mascots to her compendium of knowledge.

"You know," I admit, "I think you're a genius." It's more praise than I normally give her, usually letting our back-and-forth end with the acknowledgement that she knows things. But she is smart, and I wonder if she has a plan to get us out of our predicament. I certainly don't have a plan. I grieve for Evelyn every single day and I know Margaret does too. But if there's a way for us out of this, a way to move forward, she's the one that's going to do it.

Margaret headed north, taking the bridge over the canal to where the industrial parks were, and circled behind one of the large, non-descript warehouses to an empty lot. She stopped the car, grabbed the stick shift tight and gave me a wink. "Just like old times," she said, then floored the gas while engaging the clutch. We launched forward and she gave it even more thrust until the car just didn't feel stable to me, and with a sudden turn of the wheel Margaret shot through that instability until the car spun on smoking wheel. Margaret was laughing and I had no idea what to think. It was fun. It was cool. It just wasn't my type of thing and definitely not something I would have guessed as Margaret's thing. But surprise, here we were, and I started laughing as we come to a stop, twisted into our seats and pointed askew to the yellow parking lines.

The parking lot was wet from the recent drizzle, and Margaret took off again, riding the slick surface for all it was worth. The engine roared as the tires pounced and burnt rubber filled the air while we made our way from one end to the other, peeling out and spinning in circles over and over. At one point she pulled the parking break, trying some maneuver I would have never guessed she knew, but instead we just lurched forward and came to a stop. Margaret couldn't stop laughing. "That's probably enough," she said, "we better get out of here."

"Not in a million years."

Margaret reached over and grabbed my hand. She squeezed it and I squeezed back, and she only let go as she shifted from first to second to third on Lemont Road. I thought we were going home, until she turned right onto Bluff road, a small two-lane road that cut through the woods alongside the canal, providing a scenic view of our town and its many church spires protruding through the autumn foliage, pointing toward their heaven. I'd only been down this road once before, heard it ran down to Lockport, and that bikers liked to race along it because there were some sharp turns as well as a rise that you could catch air on if you were going fast enough. I had no doubt Margaret had heard this too.

We held hands, and Margaret kept it in third rather than shifting down as we slowed through the first gentle turn. The pavement was wet and we couldn't see if there were any oncoming cars when Margaret used the oncoming lane to loosen the turn. I didn't say anything, didn't flinch, and studied Margaret's profile. She held my hand, but besides that was concentrating fully on the road. She drove faster, and the odometer was approaching the red zone as she pushed third gear as hard as it would go. The hill was ahead, and when we hit it she loosened the gas as my stomach rolled and we momentarily left the earth, only to return with a jolt. I squeezed her hand harder, just for a second, just as something to hold onto, but also to let Margaret know I was in this with her, together.

The trees whizzed by in a blur while we passed a Deer X-ing sign, which I tried not to ignore. Another turn was ahead but Margaret didn't seem to acknowledge it, didn't slow down at all, as if we had miles of open road. This turn was sharper then the first, we were going faster, the ground was wet and I just didn't know what the Mustang could do. I didn't say anything, I trusted Margaret, but as we came into the turn I let go of her hand and braced it against the dashboard while grasping the overhead handle with my other hand. Margaret immediately released the gas, letting the engine slow us down instead of hurtling us forward, and as we came out of the turn she engaged the clutch and shifted down to second, riding the engine down to a calm, leisurely speed, allowing me a moment to catch my breath and gather my thoughts. I put my hand back on my leg, palm up, but Margaret didn't take it. She turned around shortly after and drove home, not going any faster than if we were in our old Corolla. I even reached out to take her hand, but she was busy shifting gears, turning on the radio, and the moment had passed.

But there had been a moment, and I was happy for that. For almost an entire afternoon I was happy with Margaret, happy for Margaret and happy for having Margaret. I had a moment of belief that she could pull us through our grief, somehow. If anyone could find a way to heal us, it was Margaret.

HIGH NOON

I have to use the restroom, and tell Paige, "I'll be right back," as I rise and push my chair back. I can feel my chair hit something and say without looking, "Pardon me."

"Watch your fucking self," says the large drunkard I find myself face-to-face with, once I've turned around.

"I said pardon me."

"Big fucking deal," he says, placing two fingers on my chest and pushing. He's bigger than me, there's no question about that, his stature coming from a good dose of genetic framing, a lot of weightlifting and even more beer drinking. I'm guessing he's pretty tough. Not because he'd be quick or even necessarily that good of a fighter, but because he could probably get hit by a city bus and still come at you. With a wide brow and a square chin, his shirt is pulled tight on his shoulders and chest, and even tighter on his enormous beer belly. It's an old t-shirt, falling apart at the neck and sleeves, one that may have already weathered a fight or two.

And his friends are behind him, most sitting at a table but a few standing. If anything, they look like they know their friend is an asshole and my best chance is if they hold him back. But there's also a chance they'll jump in and kick my ass too, especially if I give their friend a reason, probably any reason whatsoever, to kick my ass.

But I'm pissed too. Actually, I'm the exact opposite of pissed. I'm in a great mood on a great day after a great game talking to a great girl; that's where I am. So I'm pissed at this guy because I know he's going to ruin it. Of course if I get in a fight, I'm going to be pissed off. Even if I manage a victory, I won't be happy. And if I scuttle out of this somehow, back down with another apology, I'll spend the rest of the night pissed at myself for doing so. I'm a lean guy, probably too skinny from all the running I do, and I have no fighting experience whatsoever. But with all the beers I had through the game I think maybe I am secretly a good fighter, that somehow, out of nowhere, I might just start swinging and find myself breaking the noses of all six guys before me. Doubtful, but wouldn't it be fun?

People are watching, but no bouncers seem to notice, and there won't be any help.

"I think you and your St. Louis bitch should get the fuck out of here."

Great. I ask without trying to instigate, like it's a serious question, "Do you even know who I am?"

"No," he says, sizing me up, "and I don't give a fuck, either."

And that's when I change my tone, from tough guy to compassionate guy, the one who analyzes everything around him. "Well, it seems you do."

"What?"

"I should be absolutely nobody to you, like everyone else in here, but it seems that you're really concerned about me. Look, I accidentally bumped you with my chair, and then I immediately apologized. People are bumping into each other in this bar all the time, no big deal. Yet when I do it, you decide to be a big prick about it." I brace myself for a punch.

"So what the fuck are you going to do about it?"

"Me? Nothing. I'm just concerned why a little chair bump has you so upset. I mean, are you having a bad day today? Are you like a huge Cardinals fan and just can't handle them losing, especially to the Cubs? Is this how you show your disappointment?"

"Fuck the Cardinals."

"Hmm, that's not it. Maybe it's something bigger than that. You having some unresolved problems at work? Maybe not getting ahead like you thought? Or is it something personal? Did your girlfriend break up with you because you weren't sensitive enough? Or having trouble even finding a girl in the first place? This could be classic passive-aggressive behavior."

"Fuck you."

"Or maybe it's something even deeper. Were you picked on in kindergarten? Maybe mommy spanked you too hard, or daddy didn't spend enough time with you. You know, the whole 'cat's in the cradle' thing."

"Fuck you."

"Jeez, it may not even be something in your past. It might just be physical. Maybe you're one of those genetic oddities with two Y chromosomes and too much testosterone pumping through your body. This whole thing may not be your fault at all."

"I am so going to kick your ass."

"Look," I continue, pulling a business card out of my pocket and handing it to him. "I'm a trained psychologist and just trying to help you figure out why you can't handle a social situation like being in a bar while so many others can."

I look around, realizing the big goon is about to come after me, when a girl shouts out from a nearby table, "Take the card!" They're all laughing out loud now, and my nemesis looks at them and begins turning red with anger and embarrassment.

In a loud, yet unassuming voice, I point to the address on the card. "As you can see, I don't have a practice here in Chicago but I can definitely recommend someone locally who can help."

He comes up close, growling and snarling as he bites out a gritty warning. "You son of a bitch. I'm gonna kick your ass." And then he pushes past me and heads out the door.

I look around with eyes wide, as if puzzled why he would rush out like that. I look at his friends, and they shake their heads and sit back down. It's over, and I made it through. "Well," I say to Paige, "I really do have to go to the bathroom."

THE CASE OF THE MOVED CHEESE

When I get back, I can see everyone is looking at me. The girl who shouted at the right time, the one who saved my hide, gives me a wink and a giggle. A few other tables nod at me, and I sit down with Paige feeling like a movie star, a conquering hero, returning home.

"That was impressive," Paige says.

"Lucky."

"Have you ever used that one before?"

"What do you mean?"

"It sounded too good to be off the cuff."

"Thanks."

"I'm just saying, it sounded like a movie line, and in real life nobody ever sounds like the movies."

"Did I mention you're a smart girl?"

"Maybe in passing."

"And thanks, because it's not a movie line. A pure original, although I have thought it before. I've seen guys try to start fights like that before, and I always have found it interesting that they've never stopped to try and figure out where it stems from."

"Where the asshole gene comes from?"

"Yep. The asshole gene."

"Well," says Paige, "an impressive escape."

"Thanks."

And there I am, enjoying a perfect summer day in Chicago. The Cubs came back from a five-run deficit to win in extra innings. The sun is shining, people around me are laughing, and I just talked my way out of a fight, making the aggressor look like a complete idiot while I was a regular John Wayne. And when the next round of drinks come over, the waitress says they are already paid for, pointing to a table near us. I am amazed to find it is coming from the goon's friends. One of them, a guy of medium build, balding, and with sunburned face, starts heading our way.

"I just wanted to buy you both a drink, 'cause that was the funniest damn thing I've seen in a long time."

To the victor go the spoils. "Well thanks."

"My pleasure," he says, standing against our table and laughing some more.

"Let me ask you something," I start.

"Okay."

"That guy could have kicked the shit out of me."

"Oh no, we wouldn't have let him. He starts fights all the time. I don't know what his problem is, but after too many drinks he'll start a fight with just about anyone. That's why what you said was so funny."

"Thanks. But if you weren't here, if it were just him and me in an alley, he would have taken me, right?"

"I know he once beat up four guys at the same time. I don't know how tough they were, or exactly what happened, but I know he had no problem with them. So yeah, he would have kicked your ass."

"Great. So is he standing outside just waiting for me to leave?"

"Oh no. I'm sure he's gone home to pass out. If he even remembers this tomorrow, he'll feel like an idiot. He's actually pretty normal most of the time, besides this drunk fighting thing he's got going."

There's a pause, and then the guy pulls up a nearby chair and sits down, holding out his hand and saying, "By the way, my name is Ted."

Paige and I introduce ourselves, and now there's three.

"Did you go to the game?" Ted starts, kicking off the small talk. Yes, we did. I'm a psychologist from Georgia. Paige is a pharmaceutical sales assistant from southern Illinois, and we're both up for the weekend, up for the game, we say. We say we're friends, leaving out that we just met two days ago. I look at my watch; it's seven o'clock, and I realize it is almost forty-eight hours since I walked into the same southern Illinois bar that Paige was in.

I like this Ted guy. He's boisterous in his actions, animated in his conversation and unapologetic in his forwardness. His face is glowing red, from a combination of sunburn and too much blood going to his pale, slightly pudgy face. "So what do you do?" I ask.

"I'm a professional development trainer."

"Which is?"

"I do corporate trainings as well as seminars for individuals. Have you ever read any motivational books, like *7 Habits of Highly Effective People* or *Who Moved My Cheese?*"

"Once," I say, while Paige shakes her head no.

"I'm currently doing seminars on *Who Moved My Cheese*. It's an amazing book, just a short little fable about some mice and people in a maze, looking for cheese. It takes less than an hour to read. Yet with that book, and some training manuals, people all over the world are improving their lives, both at work and at home. It's the best selling business book of all time..."

"Ted?" I ask, stopping him mid-spiel.

"Yeah?"

"You seem like a nice guy. So I'm curious how you ended up hanging out with an asshole who likes to start fights."

"He's a good friend's roommate, high school buddies. He's a huge Cubs fan, too. So whenever my friend gets tickets, he has to invite his roommate."

"Fair enough. Carry on with your pitch."

He stops and thinks where he was. Probably exactly like he does after being interrupted in front of a large audience. It perplexes me that business executives and corporate sharks would go to this guy for motivation. But he does have a rhythm when he talks, an in-your-face sense of 'I'm excited, so let's all get excited.' And I can't help but sit back, drink my vodka gimlet, and enjoy his little show. It's interesting to find someone who's so committed to his work that he can't help falling into his spiel in a bar on a Saturday. Interesting for at least a minute or two.

"Well, the book is all about dealing with change. And what makes us happy. It's a fable that illustrates how most people are afraid of change. Paralyzed by fear when their situation does change, they continue acting in the same old ways. But the world around them, the world around us, is constantly changing, and the things that used to work stop working. The problem is that we don't accept that change and move on."

"How so?" asks Paige, who seems overly interested in our friend Ted's story.

"Well, I could even tell you the story real quick. It starts off with…"

"Since I read the homework assignment," I start, getting up from my seat, "I'm going to go to the restroom. See if there's any cheese in there."

"That's fine," says Ted, having turned his chair around so he can lean his chest against the back and get closer to Paige, pulling her into the story. "I'm sorry if this is boring, but I really believe in what I do."

"No problem," I say.

"Not enough people do," says Paige.

I don't really have to go to the bathroom, having switched from Old Style at the game to vodka gimlets now, but I empty what I can, wash my hands, grab a mint, tip the bathroom attendant and head back out. I can see Ted's arms and hands illustrating his story while Paige listens intently, as if she were listening to a mystic reading her palm or interpreting Tarot cards. She believes what Ted is telling her, falling for the trap of simplifying life's problems. To me, palm readings, Tarot cards and Who Moved My Cheese are all about the same, right about the same level as a fortune tucked inside a Chinese cookie or wrapped around a piece of Bazooka Joe bubble gum. At the very least, they get you to look at yourself, and at the very worst, they claim to have answers wrapped inside a mere sentence or two.

I ponder this at the bar, ordering myself a stiff drink, happy with how the day is going. Nothing too serious has happened, nothing to shake the foundation between Paige and me. And I feel comfortable about where things are headed. I've warned her about me, and now that that's out of the way, I can put the moves on her any way I want, because if anything does happen, it will be her own fault. 'Can't say I didn't warn ya.'

I do notice that Ted's friends seem to have gone, so it's just him and Paige talking away, except now Paige seems more animated, talking as much as he is if not more. Better head over.

"I looked everywhere," I say, taking back my seat, "but couldn't find my cheese. Somebody must have moved it."

"That happens a lot," says Ted, seriously. I always worry about people who don't know when I'm kidding.

"We were just talking about Paige's cheese," he continues. And now I laugh, unaware that he isn't kidding. "Like when Paige became pregnant in high school, that's when her cheese was moved," he tells me, deadly serious. "And rather than go looking for new cheese, she kept asking, who moved my cheese? She complained that it wasn't fair, that she deserved her original cheese, and just couldn't handle the change in her life."

I look at Paige hoping she isn't buying this, but can tell she is. "Don't you think that's an oversimplification?" I ask. "Not just of what Paige went through, but the whole story in general?"

"The story is simple, I agree with you there, but that's one of the things so fantastic about it, how such a simple little story can hold out so many truths."

"The story is about change, about dealing with it, right?"

"Exactly."

"What about when change is bad? What about when war breaks out, when disease strikes, when buses hit your loved ones crossing the street, or when they hit you? Is it just having your cheese moved and that's it?" I ask.

"Those are more extreme cases of change, but if they happen, they're still things you have to deal with."

I smile at him and don't say anything. I smile until my teeth are showing and every muscle has contracted so tight that I can't say or do anything else, because I am furious now. I'm close to leaping over the table and beating red-faced Ted to a pulp. Beating him with my fists and yelling, "Here's your fucking cheese!"

Because I know life is more complicated. I know what it's like to have terrible things happen, to have your feet knocked out from under you, to land harder than you ever thought possible, and to wonder if you'll ever get up again. And now to have some simpleton sit in front of me and tell me to deal with it, well, that's about all I can take. But I restrain myself, wordlessly, and let him go back to talking with Paige, blocking them out completely while I watch the people at the bar, try to eavesdrop on the tables behind me, and do just about anything rather than get into it with Ted.

I'm not sure what happens next. It doesn't happen because I'm drunk, although I am pretty obliterated at this point. I am slightly oblivious to my surroundings, head spinning, ignoring Paige and Ted, when I decide to go to the bathroom again. Besides wanting to walk around, I really have to go this time. I get up without saying anything, and I'm feeling better, calmer now that I've distanced myself from the whole conversation. I walk around a bit, stand in line at the bathroom, and have a chance to gather my thoughts. After pissing and washing my hands, I splash some water on my face and stare at myself in the mirror. Pull it together, I think. I dry off with a towel from the attendant, drop a dollar in the tip jar, and grab a mint on the way out. It's cool evergreen, and with it I decide I'm ready to start talking to Ted and Paige, stop wondering who moved my cheese and talk to Ted and Paige some more. It's time to get back to having fun. So after I cut through the crowds and make it back to our table, I'm slightly surprised to find it empty.

I don't think too much about it at first. I order another drink, pay for it, and remain waiting at the table, looking around from my seat, trying to figure out where they could be. And that's when it hits me. I never thought Ted could be a threat, with his pudgy red face, his exuberant mannerisms and his stupid self-help philosophies. But Paige did look interested as he gave his sales pitch. With her daughter heading off to college, she was entering a new phase of life and probably saw similarities to Ted's anecdotal mice. She probably not only fell for his who-moved-my-cheese crap, she probably fell for the idea that he believed in her, that she could start over. She probably didn't realize the moron believed in everyone, believed everything worked out for the best, and pretty much had no concept of reality.

And to top it off, she's probably still pissed at me for last night. What better way to get back at me then go off with that moron while I'm in the bathroom?

Fuck. All while I sat there and let it happen right in front of me. Fuck. Fuck. Fuck.

It's amazing how everything can go wrong during a trip to the bathroom. Two nights in a row, too. That's it; I'm done going to the bathroom. Everything seems to fall apart when I do. I'm just going to hold it in until I burst.

For a moment, just sitting there, I can feel the panic setting in. I've got to fight it off though. I order two shots of Jagermeister and close the tab. Throat burning, I take another lap around the bar, assume they must be here somewhere, but not seeing them I give up and head outside, weaving down the street on a warm dark night, people stepping aside as I swerve. Finally straightening myself by placing my hand against a glass store front, I take a moment to breathe and think, breathe and recover. With new focus, I stumble south into the city.

MY PATIENTS ARE MY FRIENDS

My patients are my friends. I mean, I am also friends with my coworkers, the doctors and the nurses and the orderlies and the janitors and the receptionists. I am friends with them as coworkers though, listening to how their weekend went, what their kids are up to, and making small talk about what's going on in the world. But I'm not close to any of them, avoiding the occasional offer to go to a bar after work, or declining the invitation to someone's Fourth of July barbecue.

But my patients, those are the people I really talk to. Or at least, they talk to me. I like them, because unlike other people, they admit right off the bat that something's wrong. They know they're depressed, that their home life's a wreck and they're afraid of what's going on in the world. They know it's all right to admit that everything's fucked up, and we can at least be comfortable with each other and our knowledge of the fucked up. My patients are the only people I've ever met who, when you ask them how they're doing, tell you.

Honestly.

"Hey John, how's it going?"
"Good. I only washed my hands twelve times this morning."
"That's great. How about you Sarah?"
"I've put on two pounds. Only two more until I hit a hundred."
"Fantastic. But remember, it's not all about the number."
"I know."
"And what about you Steve?"
"Today's not so good, doc. I want to kill everyone here."
"Hmmm. Maybe we should talk about that."

That's how it goes. I'm exaggerating, but my patients are a thousand times more open than most people. I know, I know, when you ask someone how he's doing, it's implied that you really don't want to hear his problems; it's just a friendly greeting. But you never hear the details. Everyone's walking around with fears, angers, anxieties, griefs and insecurities, but nobody ever talks about them. They hold back until these issues grow so out of control, so dominant in their lives that they end up at the hospital. It's only then when they decide, 'Hmm, maybe I should talk to someone about this?'

It's frightening too, thinking you're the only one with problems. Watching everyone with their fake smiles and insincere comments and you just want to retreat even more. That's why I'm so comforted when I get a group discussion going with a circle of perfectly nice people and realize how fucked up they are. How fucked up we all are.

That's why my patients are my friends. That's why I don't keep in contact with anyone else. That's why I've quarantined myself to a small town outside Athens, Georgia. And that's why I'm dangerous when I get out.

SEVER

I like the stories where people claim to be walking aimlessly, with no intention or direction, yet miraculously find themselves at the doorstep of their ex-lover, an old friend, or wherever they can shake their head and say, "How did I end up here?" Of course it's never a coincidence; we just pretend. We go where we know.

Which is what I'm doing. I head south from Wrigley because that's what I know of Chicago, that's where I lived. I tell myself I'm heading back to the hotel, which is true enough to let myself believe it. I head down Clark because that's where Paige and Ted left me. I turn on Sheffield because I used to walk to games along Sheffield. I turn on Lincoln because that's where the action is on a Saturday night. And I turn down Cleveland until I pass under the El and think, this is Bill and Karen's new place; the Bill and Karen whose annual rooftop barbecue used to be the best way to watch the Air and Water Show.

I've walked almost three miles, which is what I desperately needed if I'm going to hold a halfway coherent conversation. I'm going off of McCarran's directions, a block over from where they used to live, next to the El, but I know it's their place just by the landscaping. Along a street of nearly identical brick town homes, theirs is the one with no lawn. Instead, tiers of landscaping containing flowers and vines and bushes I could never name, all surround what looks like a Koi pond, though I don't see any giant fish. It's the exact landscaping I would expect from Bill and Karen. The lights are on, so I knock twice on the red door and wait.

"No way," exclaims the thin man opening the door, holding a large glass of red wine in one hand while he readjusts his stylish glasses with the other.

"Hello Bill," I say.

"Not in a million years," he starts, then turns back and yells into his house, "guess who's here?" Turning back he waves me in, and I enter, all smiles.

And there in the front living room are Pete and Megan, Ray and Stacy, and Bill's wife Karen, who just walked in from the kitchen holding a bottle of wine. The place is immaculate, as always, with cushy leather sofas and antique wooden furniture adorning the front room. A large picture of the Chicago skyline is on the opposite side. I know it was taken by Bill on some

New Year's sunrise, photography being one of his top twenty hobbies. His number one hobby is blowing up his pictures, or displaying his collection, or making some sort of exhibit, and then telling everyone what he likes about his work. Bill always was an enormous blow hard, and I'm sure still is, which was a trait that could be hard to put up with if it weren't so much fun to ridicule. McCarran, whom I don't see anywhere and probably stopped coming years ago, always called him 'Blow-Hard Bill.' Only half the time would he accompany it with a blow-job gesture.

And everyone looks the same. Older, strangely austere in my presence, but the same. I walk around the room, shaking hands and getting hugs, all done in slow motion, emphasizing how long it's been.

"You look great," Megan says, "so athletic."

"I run," I say, "quite a bit."

"It's good to have a hobby," Karen says, "it's so good for you."

I smile and nod, glad she knows what's good for me. I smile with teeth clenched, ensuring the 'fuck you' doesn't spill out.

"McCarran mentioned he saw you yesterday, but we didn't really think you'd make it."

"What, miss B&K's AAWB? Never." Their parties used to have such elaborate names we started going to acronyms. The Bill and Karen Annual Air and Water Show Barbecue. I think I'm close enough. Regardless, just another way to make fun of them and avoid that I've missed quite a few of these parties. I haven't seen these people in five years. Since a funeral. And yet here I am, out of the blue. Surprise!

"Right. It's only been, let's see…" starts Bill, looking to the ceiling as he tries to figure it out.

"Let's not worry about it," I say.

"Wine?" offers Karen, and I take her up with a greedy smile, positioning myself at the end of one of the couches, next to Ray and Stacy.

There's the obligatory moment of silence now that whatever idle conversation had been going on is no longer relevant. I take this moment to look around, and I can't help thinking, these were my friends? I don't even know what to say.

"So what have you been up to?" asks Pete, sitting on the other couch with Megan, holding hands.

"Same job, same place. Not much new to report."

"And you still like it down there, in… where is it again?"

"Georgia."

"That's right."

"It treats me well."

Pause. Awkwardness.

"So," I start, "where is everyone? These things used to be packed until midnight."

117

"The suburbs," says Stacy. "Most everyone's moved to the suburbs. They all have kids and baby-sitters and soccer practice tomorrow, so they come by for a few hours and head back before nightfall."

"A damn shame," says Bill, shaking his head. "You're looking at a dying breed, the last of the city folk. Although we're not giving in to the suburbs, even when we do decide to have kids, right babe?"

"Right," says Karen, with an accepting smile, setting her drink on the cherry wood coffee table and folding her hands in her lap.

"Way to continue the fight," I say, unsure if I'm happy for them or disgusted. I'm happy because they're resisting building a family, putting all their eggs in one basket. I'm happy because they might be able to avoid what I've been through. But I'm disgusted because I'm human. "So what have I missed?"

And first I hear about the people who have moved to the suburbs, who were sitting in this room earlier today. I hear about how many kids they have and where they live, but I think that's all they know or remember about their suburban friends, the basic facts. Then they tell me about themselves. I hear about job promotions, vacations to distant lands, theatre productions they've seen, and their last good meal. Bill and Karen always have an assortment of quirky hobbies, and are currently doing glassblowing. They point out the works on the mantelpiece, the ones I wondered about since they are so out of place. Bloated glass in brilliant colors, like mutant fish pulled up from the depths of an ocean trench, things that should have never been exposed to sunlight.

"Lovely," I say.

"How do you like the wine?" Bill asks. And this usually would be an in for him to tell me about it, what vineyard and vintage it's from, and what unique way it was grown or crushed or mixed or aged or bottled or how it was the perfect match to such and such, which may be true now, but it's also because I've finished my glass, had Karen pour me another one, and have almost finished that one. I can sense their wondering eyes, carefully watching as I down each glass, listening to my already slurred speech. But as long as I maintain my composure, say things like 'Lovely,' without laughing, I'll be fine.

"It's from Argentina," continues Bill. "Karen and I went there last winter and toured the wineries. Very quaint. It was a fantastic trip."

"Sounds lovely."

"That red you're drinking there, it's a Trapiche Merlot-Malbec. 1997. We toured their plantation, walked beside the fields this exact bottle was made from. We even ate dinner with the owner, just him, his wife, Karen and I."

"Lovely," I say.

"Here, let me show you something." Bill gets up and I follow him down the hallway. "We're doing a South American theme in our back room." He opens the door to a room filled with a multitude of trinkets, vases, artwork and other items I don't recognize. "Everything in here we bought in South America. Most of it's Argentinian, but we also have a lot of Chilean, Bolivian and Brazilian items. And it's all authentic, bartered for on the streets and in the markets."

I look around, trying to take it in and show appreciation, but I have no idea what to say. 'Lovely' is not the right word.

"Here," Bill says, bending over and holding up the light blue carpet in his fingers, "this is one-hundred percent alpaca wool. We bought it from an old woman near San Miguel de Tucumán. She was an amputee, with no legs." Bill runs his finger along the ziggurat patterns, and I'm almost embarrassed at how humorous I find the idea of a legless woman's life skill is making carpets for others to walk on. Almost, but not quite. "And this painting, we bought it in Alta Italia from the town elder. He claimed to be a hundred years old, but nobody's sure because there are no birth certificates."

I study the painting. What appear to be teeth, giant ivory teeth, jut out from the right side, the lips pursed back in a scowl. I can't tell if they belong to something human or not. The sun is sinking in the background, and one tree lies on its side, torn from the ground with its roots hanging listlessly in the air. Once again, 'lovely' is not the right word.

I am shown some more trinkets and can't help wonder how Bill became my friend, or when he went off the deep end. He always had side hobbies and interests that came up in conversation. I remember when this was the Tokyo room, with rice paper on the walls, pictures and carvings of dragons and samurai on the shelves, strange little boxes cluttered throughout. But before he lived here, before he got married, I think Bill was almost normal. I remember him watching sports with the rest of the guys, going down to the beach and looking for girls in bikinis, going to bars and drinking the cheap beer.

"Wow," I say, wondering what the hell happened. I want to get out of this room. "Mind if I go up to your rooftop? I'd like to see the skyline again."

"Sure. Here, let me get some more wine and we'll head up." He reappears with a new bottle and I fill my own glass. My head's spinning, and for some reason I think more wine will do the trick.

I follow Bill up the stairs, through the back bedroom's sliding glass door onto the back porch, and then up more stairs to a small rooftop deck. I look around, not just taking in the scenery, but intently looking for something east of us.

"What are you looking for?" asks Bill.

"A steeple."

"A steeple?"

"Yep."

"Any one in particular?" he asks. There are numerous church steeples rising from the various neighborhoods around us.

Not until I see it, just one that catches my fancy. "That one right there," I say, pointing off across the horizon.

"Where?"

"That dome with the cross sticking up and the small ring beneath it."

"Ahh, right there? I see it. What about it?"

"Do you know where it is?"

Bill thinks while I try to get my bearings. It's northwest of us, probably a mile or so. "I think I've seen the church, but I don't know the name of it or anything."

"Do you know what street it's on?"

"That's Bucktown, probably around Milwaukee and Armitage. Maybe not quite all the way out there. Why?"

"Just curious," I say.

"Is everything all right?"

"Couldn't be better," I say, an obvious lie.

"Are you ever going to move back?"

"I don't know," I say. "Not anytime soon. It's better for me down there."

I finish my wine with one good swallow and find the bottle sitting on a wrought iron table, next to a burning candle. I refill my glass and look around, this time taking everything in. It's peaceful up here, somehow slowing down the rush of the city with this aerial perspective. I remember the parties, standing on the deck at their old place, full of people, friends, friends of friends, strangers, all forming circles of conversation, mingling and laughing without a care.

"Are you happy?" I ask Bill.

"Definitely," he says without thinking about it. "Without a doubt."

"Do you ever feel…," I start. I pause because I don't want to hurt his feelings.

"Feel what?"

"Hollow?" I say.

And he does think about the question, but only pauses to let me know he's thinking about it. He puts his hand on my shoulder and say, "It's all right. No matter how you feel, it's all right."

I didn't mean me, you jackass. I wasn't saying I felt hollow and I wasn't looking for sympathy. You are, Bill. Hollow. Shallow. Inane. Frivolous. But I continue leaning on the railing, hunched over my elbows, taking in the city around me. I'll give him the benefit of the doubt that he assumes I'm talking about myself because I'm the one crying.

"Well, I found what I wanted, or at least a good start. Milwaukee and

Armitage. Let's go join the others." I wipe my eyes and follow Bill downstairs.

We join the others in the living room, where they're talking about the stock market, what's hot and what's not, which leads to phone companies and who makes the coolest phone. Blackberries versus the Motorola RAZR, and how someday we'll all have a cell phone in our pocket, so every company's going to be a winner. They move to the latest cars they like, a category that seems restricted to BMWs and Mercedes. I sit deeply in the couch, listening and watching, wondering what I'm doing here. The conversation turns to summer homes, not that anyone has one, but it probably won't be long as they discuss traits they would like in one, proximity to the beach, places with trendy neighbors, distance from the city. I envision Bill and Karen going first, as they both have good jobs and plenty of money. Conversations about their lake house and how they're decorating it and what big party they're planning and who they're inviting up. Full weekends of figuring out what's in season and what dinner to make from what's in season and what wine to pair with the dinner of what's in season, of sitting outside around a fire while waves crash in the distance and smoke intermingles with the briny air, when someone eventually fills a gap in the conversation by saying how lucky they all are. Fuck! This whole scene is not just a possibility but a near certainty, a certainty I can't take. I get up and head towards the bathroom, swaggering and bleary eyed, giving everyone a nod as I go.

On my way here I thought it funny how people go for a walk and claim serendipity when they mysteriously end up at the one place they probably wanted to go to from the beginning. As if it just happened out of nowhere that they took the correct turns, miraculously finding themselves at the doorstep of their ex-lover. I said it didn't really happen that way.

It might be possible with a few drinks though. Or a ton of Saturday-afternoon-at-a-Cubs-game drinks. Especially when the mistake is not walking through the many streets outside, choosing a new direction at every intersection, but when it's simply missing the first door on your right, which is the bathroom, and going into the second door. It's an easy mistake. Which is why, when I hear my name called out, I'm surprised to open my eyes and find myself not in the bathroom but in the Argentinean room, one hand pressed squarely against the teeth picture, pissing on the blue alpaca rug bought from a legless lady near San Miguel de Tucumán.

"What the hell are you doing?" yells Karen.

"Oh shit," I say, looking down in surprise as I continue my business.

"Stop that! Please!"

"Just a minute." Man, I must have been holding back for a while, because I just keep going. And having removed my hand from the wall, I can't help but sway a little, spreading it around.

"Jesus!" yells Bill, who now stands behind his wife, gathered with everyone else in the doorway.

I shake twice, tuck it away, zip up and head towards the living room, half wondering where I am and half knowing exactly where I am.

"I can't believe you just did that," says Pete, who I can tell almost wants to laugh if he weren't so embarrassed for me.

"Did what?" I look around like I just misplaced something. "Where's my wine? That's pretty good stuff Bill."

"You did that on purpose," says Stacy, who always was a smart girl. "You just pissed on their best rug, their favorite rug, on purpose."

"Stacy…"

"I know you did." And as Stacy thinks about it, she needs to qualify it, like everything in life. "That is so wrong."

"I can't believe you just…" starts Bill.

I'm still looking around. "I can't find my wine glass."

"Stop fucking around! Jesus Christ! You need serious help. I mean something's wrong with you."

And that's when I maybe become a little defensive. "Something's wrong with me? What about you, you and your stupid precious little South American room? I wish I could have taken a shit in there."

"Are you insane?"

"And all this crap," I say, "all this photography of yours and these ugly, ugly glass blown thingies. What is all this supposed to be?"

"Can we just stop this?" cries out Karen.

"It's called art," says Bill, willing to defend himself. "It's called culture."

"It's called hiding. Spending your whole life, following one insignificant whim after another, and never following anything real, anything important."

"Stop this," says Karen, "Stop this right now!"

"But I can't blame you. Not relying on anything. I can't blame you at all. I guess no matter what happens, no matter how often someone pisses on your rug, you'll be all right. Just keep putting your faith in things that don't matter."

"I will not let you come into my home and insult me like this!"

"I think you better go," says Ray approaching, trying to escort me to the door.

"Like you Ray, at least they're not living precariously like you." As I say this, I can feel the devilish grin spreading across my face.

"What? Just go," he commands.

"I'm just saying, if Stacy ever found out about that stripper you brought home when she was at that yoga retreat in Sedona…"

And with that comment everyone freezes.

I pull my arm away from Ray, who can't turn around to face Stacy, but can only stare at me wondering how I just said what I did, how he's going to deny it.

"And Pete, did you finally ever tell Megan about those sales bonuses, or do you still gamble them all away? I'm guessing by now, Megan's lake house has been lost at the craps table." I take one look around the room, at the wide-eyed, slack-jawed expressions, and wonder which is worse. Finding out you've lost your husband's fidelity, or finding out you've lost your summer cottage on Lake Michigan. In this room, I could take a pretty good guess.

With that I turn and open the door. Nobody says anything, but I can hear Megan start to sob. I turn back towards them to say one last parting shot, but find myself losing balance as I trip over their welcome mat. I somehow spin around and catch myself, enough to land on my hands and knees, and stare at the concrete while I gather myself. The door slams shut with their last view that will become their last memory of me lying there, pathetically crouched over, confirming that whatever I said were the words of a pathetic man. Use that image when defending yourself, when laying the foundation of your self-denial. But just because I'm pathetic does not mean I'm lying.

I crawl back up, clutching a flower pot and pulling it to the floor, crashing beneath me. "I'm all right," I shout through the door, knowing nobody cares, knowing nobody believes that I am all right. I hear the voices flaring up inside, the accusations, the denials, and understand I have severed all ties with these people, forever.

ON A ROLL

I head south, towards the hotel, and I can't help thinking this is Paige's fault. If she hadn't left with red-faced Ted, I would have never come here. That was her one duty this weekend, to keep me in control. I don't think that's asking for too much. I'm surprisingly furious, and she's the only one I can blame.

Of course I shouldn't be mad. I know she's trying her best, doing what she thinks is best. But if I make it back to the hotel and find her and Ted all snuggled up in my bed, well, let's just say everyone at Bill and Karen's will consider themselves lucky in comparison. I'd never be violent, that's not who I am, but I can certainly cause a scene. Turns out I'm really good at that. But I don't want to think about them now. I just want to concentrate on my walking, getting back to the hotel and sleeping, confident that one day this will all be a half-forgotten memory.

Of course, heading south from Bill and Karen's place takes me right through the heart of Cabrini Green, which is probably not a good place for a wasted single white guy to be walking at 2 a.m. Sunday morning. Although nobody on the streets seems to be bothering me, I am suddenly very conscious of my surroundings.

The public housing buildings look burnt out and cold in the blue lights that illuminate their facade. The rooms seem empty. I wonder what it would be like to have a spotlight always shining into your front window. I can see a few people standing in the shadows, a few congregating around a dumpster and a few more near an old silver Buick. I walk ignorantly beneath the streetlights, allowing everyone to see the color of my skin, the stumble in my walk, and the bluster in my stride. I feel up for anything tonight.

After passing a few buildings, two black guys do approach me, one with a shopping cart and the other with his hand outstretched. "Hey there, how ya doing on this beautiful night?" He's all smiles and pitch, and I feel like he's approaching me on a used car lot rather than the middle of Cabrini in the dark quiet of night. I shake his hand, prepared for something to happen, and then just try to keep walking.

"Hey, hey, hey. Where ya going? We got a little proposition for you. Why don't you hear me out?"

I stop and listen. I want to be more convivial then confrontational. The one behind the shopping cart says nothing. His clothes are ragged and worn, definitely from Goodwill, while the one talking seems to be dressed better, wearing relatively new tennis shoes, jeans and a blue polo. That worries me more, since that means he bought them and that means he's getting money from somewhere, or someone. I wonder if drunk white guys wander into this area on a regular basis, like ships in the Bermuda triangle. In my drunken state I wonder if I can take them, since they're both a little shorter than me, which I somehow think gives me an advantage.

I want to fight. I may even want to lose. But I smile and listen for now.

"We're selling some champagne here, and I was wondering if you'd be interested?" He pulls a bottle out of the cart and holds it out to me at a tilt, resting it against his forearm, as if he wanted me to check the label and make sure it was the bottle I ordered. I recognize it as a cheap brand stocked in most grocery stores. There's no way it's worth more than five dollars.

I wonder how many white guys wander here in the middle of the night looking for champagne. I'm pretty sure it's not enough to run a business. I'm either going to get jumped from behind or these two are going to take care of me themselves. But fuck it. I'm looking to fight.

I take the bottle from his hand and look at it closely. "That's good stuff," he says, at which I turn the bottle so I'm holding it like a club and step towards him as I slowly swing the bottle at him.

He jumps back, although my swing is so far off he doesn't have to. "Come on you mother fuckers!" I shout.

"Hey, hey buddy. Settle down there."

"Don't give me that shit, I know what you're up to." I step towards the pitchman and take another swing at him, again missing by a mile, although this time I almost lose my balance. I can see the cart man has backed up about ten paces, almost frightened, and the pitchman starts moving back on his own too.

"Calm down," he says, holding his hands up, palms out. "Calm down."

"Fuck you! Bring it on."

But they won't. They just keep backing away like frightened kids when daddy gets drunk. And I hear the one with the cart, the one with the used clothing and haggard look mutter, "He's crazy."

"You're damn right I am!" And that's the strangest part. There are two guys selling cheap champagne in the middle of Cabrini Green a few hours before sunrise, and I'm the crazy one.

"We're just trying to sell something, man. Trying to make a living."

"Aren't we all," I say. I take out my wallet and take out all the money and throw it in the cart. I don't count it, but it's more than a hundred and less than two hundred. "How's that?" I ask. It suddenly occurs to me that I may be in a drug deal, maybe Champagne is something else. I just don't know. They're grabbing all the wadded up bills, straightening them out. I slip off my sandals and flip them towards the cart, standing barefoot. I take the bottle of champagne and heave it down the street, as far as I can. It makes a popping noise as it explodes across the pavement, and I can't tell if it sounds more like gunshots or fireworks, if we're fighting or celebrating. I decide it's a gunshot, a blank, used to start the race, and take off at full speed, barefoot, through the point of impact.

"That's one crazy dude," I hear, unsure if it's the voice of the two salesmen, or just a voice in my head. I run barefoot back to the hotel, refusing to look down, refusing to watch my step, pretending I'm one of those serious barefoot runners, like this is normal. I ignore the pain in my feet, and ignore the creeping idea that this may take a while to heal, may prevent me from running back home, and I'm not sure what I'll do without that release.

Paige is in the room, nestled alone in her cot, and the hotel bed is wrapped tight once again. I throw the pillows off the bed and slide my bloody feet into the white crease, like a giant bandage, and let go into a dreamless sleep.

TWO SHEETS OF DRYWALL

It was the last game of the season. That's the only baseball detail I remember. I think the Cubs were playing Milwaukee, but it could have been St. Louis. It was a Sunday and I was lying on the couch. It was a dismal season, which was appropriate for the worst year of my life. If the Cubs were winning, celebrating as they tried to make the postseason, I'm not sure I could have watched. Instead, they went through the motions, tried to get their hits in, made their plays, and tried to finish with a bit of respectability. Wait 'til next year. That I could handle. Their season was pretty much already over when Evelyn passed, and yet they had months of games to play, games I could watch that meant nothing, and I was grateful for that.

Margaret said she was going somewhere. I wish I could remember what she said, but I don't. Her actual words, her tone, what she did with her hands, what her eyes conveyed, how long she looked at me, I don't remember any of it. She had been going on long drives ever since she got the Mustang and I was no longer invited. My hope that Margaret might find a way out for us had passed. I was just as bad as ever, crying in the morning while finding the days too long, too slow, and too empty. Margaret didn't seem happier, either. If she came back from her long drives rejuvenated, perhaps happy, I would be happy for her. Most of the time when she came back, I could tell she'd been crying too. Careening around who knows where, reliving one of the high points of her youth with tears in her eyes. I wondered if she went back to Bluff Road and continued ripping through those tight turns, flying over the hill, much the way we had on our first trip. I worried she was going to kill herself, but I never said anything. The effort for a difficult conversation was a mountain too high to climb. She just disappeared for a few hours and then she'd be back.

This trip wasn't different from any of her previous trips. Margaret told me she was going, headed to the garage, and I didn't think anything else about it. Although the door to the garage was just past the front hall, the actual garage shared a wall with our family room, the same wall I was staring at, watching the Cubs go through the motions. I heard her open the door to the garage. I think I said goodbye. I think. But I didn't think about what was missing. I heard the car start and went back to watching my game, but I never heard the garage door. It's obvious now, that the garage door had to open for Margaret to go anywhere, but I wasn't listening. And what I just said isn't necessarily true; she could go somewhere.

I had finished one beer over eight innings. I didn't really drink anymore, at least not in the way I used to, but wasn't quite ready to say I was done drinking, throwing a six pack into my grocery cart now and then, not really caring what it was. I grabbed one of those beers at the start of the Cubs game and probably finished two-thirds of it. Habit. Or maybe just one of those things I thought a proper Cubs fan was supposed to do. It grew warm and flaccid, and yet I occasionally reached up and let the liquid touch my lips. I treated the bottle more like a lip balm than a beer. An occasional swig that would fester in my mouth while I watched a few practice swings, a pitch down the middle hit foul, just stuff happening. If anything, the beer kept me from falling to my side and curling up on the couch. It kept me upright.

After a few hours I rose, poured the remains down the drain, threw the bottle into the recycle bin and went to the bathroom. I think. This day is strangely foggy, a dense dream-state that I sometimes wonder if any of what I remember really happened. I probably poured out that beer, threw it in the recycling bin, and then went to the bathroom, but I may not have. The only reason I would have gone to the garage was to get another beer, and that's why I assume I finished that first one. Something to do.

Wait 'til next year. I do remember that. The announcers were quoting the Cubs unofficial slogan, indirectly acknowledging a horrible season while holding out that glimmer of hope that if you just wait 'til next year, things might get better. Emphasize the good players who hopefully wouldn't get traded. Bring up the few small things that need improvement. Pitching, hitting and some fielding. Talk about the great prospects coming up through their farm league, unseen talent that the casual observer couldn't disagree with. They wove a good story, a good enough story, that most of us could nod, purse our lips and agree that yeah, next year just might be the year. Of course most of the time it was said as a joke, with almost a century of wait-'til-next-years having been passed through the generations, a joke about hope that was really about lost hope. I don't know if I necessarily believed it, but I do remember thinking it was nice. Hope. Wait 'til next year. Just wait 'til next year, one foot in front of the other, and maybe pretty-please next year will be better.

I turned the garage door handle, pushed and immediately knew. Margaret still sat up, yet seemed to be caving in on herself. Her head tilted to the side, trying to pull her over, yet maybe she was looking for something in the center console. Her hair still looked pretty, still fell to the sides of her face the way that would normally cause her to casually brush it back, that easy gesture that reminded me that I loved this woman. She didn't brush her hair back. The garden hose was taped to the exhaust and ran through the passenger window, a beach towel stuffed alongside to fill the gap. Swirls of red and black, I had seen her lie on that towel poolside in Cabo, in her green bikini, big black sunglasses on, reading. I'm not sure why that towel was used, but there it was, holding the carbon monoxide inside Margaret's red Mustang hard-top.

I need to be honest with myself. Margaret did have a Mustang convertible when she was a kid and buying one now was meant to be a treat, a trip down memory lane. But if Margaret bought herself a treat, she would have gone all the way and bought herself a convertible. That was how Margaret worked. She bought the hard-top with this day in mind. Margaret was always two steps ahead. She always had a game plan. And she always had a strong follow through.

When I found Evelyn, I ran to her. I did everything I could to revive her. I wasn't going to wait 'til next year. But I just stood staring at Margaret, unsure what to do. It may have only been a minute, I have no idea, but I just stood and pondered, and to be honest, I grew a bit angry. Angry at Margaret for tricking me into thinking she had turned a corner, had gone out and purchased something that might make her happy, for tricking me into believing she was even trying to find a way to move forward.

Being truthful about it all, here's what I think happened. Margaret sped down Bluff Road that rainy day, engine roaring while the tires used every last tread to grip the road, and I don't think she meant to kill us that day, but she was asking what I thought about the possibility. Would I join her? When we did that final swerve through that tight turn, as my body pressed against the door, I let go of her hand and grabbed the console. It was just a reaction. I didn't mean anything by it, just an involuntary grasp. I didn't know I was being tested. I didn't know I was being asked a question.

I wasn't angry at Margaret for killing herself. That made sense. That I understood. But after we swore to stick together, for better or for worse, I was angry at Margaret for not inviting me along. I wouldn't have protested. I wouldn't have asked questions. I would have sat there patiently, sanguinely listening to her tape the hose to the exhaust. I would have raised the window while she held the other end of the hose and beach towel in place. I might have pressed play on the tape deck. I most definitely would have held her hand for the entirety of our trip.

Margaret was always the strong one, the one who got things done, and as such, she was supposed to invite me, her husband, the father of her child, to accompany her. But Margaret didn't invite me, and so there I was. The weak one, who laid on the couch and watched baseball, not recognizing that if I just looked beyond the TV, the drywall and the 2" x 4"s, I would have watched my wife's suicide. I would have stood at the Departures window and watched Margaret leave me to join Evelyn. Leaving me, the weak one, all alone.

RECAP

I hurt all over. It's dark here, buried beneath the covers, and my head pounds just listening to the hum of the room's air conditioning. My stomach is held tight, wretched and empty. My feet burn and I'm afraid to look at them. I remember a bottle of Champagne, the sound of it bursting open, replaying again and again in my head, like a fireworks finale. My only relief, my only way to confirm I am still alive, is to listen to myself calling out in a long guttural cry, "Mmmmuuuuuuuuugggggghhhhh!"

I listen, but there is no response. I turn, curling forward like a potato bug, trying to stretch out the knot that has so prominently formed in my back. I call out again.

And again, no response.

So I pull the covers down around me until light fills my cave. I poke my head out, confirming I am alone. The bedside clock reads 10:30 and the room is empty. The cot along the wall has been made up, a towel hangs on the back of the chair, and I can tell the bathroom door is open and the light is off. I wonder if Paige left me.

But she can't be mad at me. Anything and everything bad I did was after she disappeared on me. Paige is the one who decided to run off with king cheese-head to who-knows-where to do who-knows-what. Son of a bitch, I mumble to myself, more upset at being alone than at anything she did. I pull myself down to the floor and crawl to the mini-fridge. I open it and see a bottle of Champagne. I grab it and crawl back into bed, unwrap the tinfoil at the top, unwind the mousetrap beneath, and pop the cork. It's astringent and my throat closes down, but it's bubbly, it's cold and it's alcohol, and that's good enough. As long as it's alcohol the rest doesn't matter.

I sit and sip for ten minutes, thinking more about what I have to do today than what happened yesterday, about burying the Target Box, driving home afterwards, about being alone. Before any of that I have to manage to get out of bed. There are streaks of red across the sheets, so I eventually twist my right foot up and survey the bottom. Scraped and bruised, but not too bad. I switch to my left foot and find a large gash across the pad beneath my big toe, a crescent scar with dried blood, but I don't see any glass. I think I got lucky, although it's amazing how shitty being lucky can feel. I finally get out of bed and awkwardly heel walk to the bathroom to piss. For the first time I notice Paige's bags packed and placed by the door. So she's coming back. Good. I shower, dry off, and put some old bandages and gauze from my dopp kit onto both feet. If I wear socks and my running shoes, I should be able to get around fine. But no running for a while.

I order room service, a double cheeseburger, fries, and an order of fries on the side. My system is so far from normal that I can barely think straight. I make the bed in order to hide the blood stains, and I pack my bags to gain some semblance of order and control. Last night's events reappear like lightning flashes and I don't feel guilty; I don't feel guilty as long as they remain nothing more than flashes, as long as I don't concentrate on what I did and who I am.

The champagne isn't any better with lunch, but I finish three-fourths of the bottle before taking it into the bathroom. I don't want to get wasted today, but my hands are shaking and my eyes are having trouble adjusting between the room's darkness in the bathroom and light pouring in the cracked drapes. I take one last swig and then pour the rest down the drain. I get out mouthwash and rinse, spit and then rinse it along the sink, trying to overpower the smell. I put the bottle back into the refrigerator and close it, hopefully hiding my misdeeds.

I'm lying on the bed when the door opens and Paige enters. It's almost 1:00. She looks relieved to see me up and all of our bags packed by the door. She gives a scowl at the sight of the Target Box sitting on the desk. We look at each other with questions. Paige starts, "So what happened to you last night?"

"I think that's the question I should be asking you."

"What do you mean?"

"I went to the bathroom for a minute, and when I got back, you and that Ted guy had taken off."

"We didn't leave."

"Well I was there at our table, all by myself."

"We were dancing."

"Dancing?"

"Yes. I told Ted that I liked to dance, so he showed me the dance floor. When we got there, they were playing a song I liked, so we danced a bit and came back. You were already gone."

"There's no dance floor at John Barleycorn."

"Do you think I'm making this up?" she asks.

"Well, I lapped the entire bar and there was not a dance floor. I looked all over for you."

"Did you go upstairs?"

I have to ponder. "Upstairs?"

"Yes, upstairs."

"There wasn't an upstairs."

Paige's eyes bead up. She's sick of me, there's no doubt about it, and I sound like a petulant kid, accusing her of lying rather than admitting my own mistakes, and I was clearly making mistakes last night.

"I didn't see an upstairs."

"The entire second floor is a dance floor. Loud speakers, flashing strobe lights, a DJ in the corner and wall-to-wall dancing. Including us."

"Hmmm," I mutter, chewing on this new information. They didn't ditch me. And John Barleycorn, which is decorated like an old English bar, with large wooden beams overhead, model ships and paintings of stuffy Englishmen on the walls, also has a techno dance floor right above it. I can't trust anything anymore.

"So back to my question. What happened to you? You didn't get home until 3:00 A.M."

"You were up?"

"I wasn't, but your mumbling woke me. I could hear you panting too, like you'd been running from something."

I'd rather think about the stairs leading up. I don't remember seeing any, but did see a large group congregating just off the front door. People could come in and go directly upstairs, completely skipping the old-time bar feel on the first floor. That must have been where Paige and Ted went upstairs, without inviting me. Damn I feel like a baby.

"Well?"

"I walked around for a while. Then stopped by that party McCarran mentioned."

"Your friend's party?"

"Yeah," I say, "my friend's party," glad that the word friend doesn't have a past tense.

"How was it?"

"Interesting."

"That's good. It's good to visit friends."

"Yes, it can be." Paige looks like she's waiting for me to expand on the subject, that she'll ask a question if I don't, so I stand up and try not to wince as my feet touch the floor. "Ready to check out?"

We load up the car, and I suggest going to the Air and Water Show. We've listened to them buzz overhead for the past two days, so I figure we might as well actually watch some of it. We park on Cleveland near Lincoln Avenue, which I realize is within walking distance of Bill and Karen's condo, and then head toward the North Avenue Beach, following families and couples with lawn chairs under their arms and coolers slapping against their sides. Once again, the weather is perfect, upper eighties with a steady breeze. Paige wears brown shorts and a lacy navy blue top. She walks calmly by my side, but thirty years have passed between us. No longer are we the

132

budding couple getting to know each other, and instead find there is nothing we can say that will pique the other's interest, and what feels like years of slights and imperfections have solidified our relationship. After two days, Paige can barely tolerate me, and I'm thankful for that.

"So where did you go this morning?"

"I ate at some place called Stanley's."

"Ahh, the breakfast buffet."

"You've been there?"

"Many times. A good place to stuff yourself after a night of drinking."

"Mission accomplished."

"Did you go alone?"

"I met Ted there."

"So," I start. "You and Ted."

"What about it?"

"You like him?"

"He's nice."

"So what do you like about him?"

"He's nice. He's fun to talk to. He's interesting and genuine."

"Just like me."

"I'm not answering that."

"What?"

"You know that you are only interested in yourself. That's become more than apparent."

And I think about it. Paige is wrong on that point, but I understand why she would think it. It's not that I don't care for other people, but I'm frightened for them. Too frightened. I know what can happen in this world. But if she thinks I'm vain, that's probably close enough. "Possibly," I respond, not caring to change her mind.

We find a spot along the grass, a few feet up from the sidewalk and beach. This allows us to sit back and relax between fly-bys, much more natural than standing and trying to think of things to say to fill the gaps. I take my shoes off to let my feet rest. They've been burning the whole time, though the champagne helped.

"Your foot's bleeding," Paige points out.

I look down, feigning surprise. "A blister," I say. "I shouldn't have run on it yesterday."

Paige listens but doesn't really care.

Apache helicopters perform synchronized aerials along the waterfront. Biplanes release their smoke machines as they roll off one by one, drawing loops in the sky. A jet fighter shoots past in a streak of excitement, followed by the sonic boom that gets the crowds cheering. The jets are everyone's favorite, with their power and speed as they touch both sides of the horizon in mere seconds, disrupting the very nature of sound in its course.

I love the jets, but my favorite act starts right after. A single, simple biplane, painted yellow with red tipped wings, starts off with a few barrel rolls. It turns upward, gently increasing its angle of ascent, slowing down as the engine drives upward, until eventually it stops in midair for a moment, as if painted on the horizon, before the engine stalls out and the plane falls gently onto its back, rolls and flails while plummeting toward Lake Michigan. After four seemingly out-of-control flops where everyone thinks it's getting too close to the lake, a moment after the crowd thinks, *that's enough playing around*, the bi-plane regains control and climbs up from the horizon.

While rising, the plane rolls to its side so we can see the top, see the man strapped into the open cockpit. Fighting against gravity, it slows down and eventually loses its grip in the sky, the front end falling down like a clock arm hinged at the tail, which holds steady, until it releases into another freefall, another haphazard drop before regaining control. For fifteen minutes these falling pirouettes of disaster continue. The plane is practicing controlled chaos. Never getting too high or too low, just forcing itself into tailspins and stalls and head-over-heel rollovers, pulling out and demonstrating that it was in control the whole time. Ta-da. This stunt plane is different than every other act, not trying to impress us with harmony, speed, or a mastery of the skies. No, this plane touches on nihilism, teases us with the wonderment of losing control, and lets us wonder if it's always possible to recover and avoid the eternal disaster.

Symbolism at its finest.

EVER AFTER

"So when are you going to bury that thing?" asks Paige, holding a burrito with both hands. I sit across from her in the booth, having decided to hit Taco Burrito Joint #2 for dinner, something simple, quick and good. I'm on my third beer.

"Tonight."

"It better be tonight. I'm supposed to be at work tomorrow."

"You'll probably want to sleep in the car."

"Great."

"So you'll be a little tired." She can't respond because her mouth is full, which gives me a chance to talk. "You know Paige, I wanted to thank you for coming along with me. It's probably not been what you expected, but I appreciate it."

"No," she gets out, then holds up a finger while she chews and eventually swallows. "It's not at all what I expected. But it was an adventure. And I had some fun."

"Glad to hear that."

"So can I ask you again?"

"Ask me what?"

"What's in the Target Box?"

"As I've said, I don't know."

"For once I'm going to pretend you're not lying to me and you really have no idea, but then what's the point? Why drive it to Chicago and bury it?"

"That's a good question. And at least partially, it's an excuse to go to Chicago. It gives me a reason."

"Why do you need a reason? People go on vacation and visit a city all the time. That's what I did, and I didn't need to have some mystical, made-up Target Box for me to do so."

"It's not made up," I say. "It's not just an excuse to come up here. It's a reason, a purpose, a real purpose. Whether there's anything in there or not, whether it's all just…"

"All just what?"

"I don't know, Paige, I really don't know."

"When you first showed me the Target Box, I really wanted to know what was in it. I was surprised how curious I was. But now, now that I know you, now that the weekend is over, I really just don't care anymore."

"Thanks."

"Well?"

"And who said it's over?"

"What do you mean?"

"Feel like listening to some jazz?"

She thinks for a minute and I'm surprised by her response. "Possibly."

"How about we head over to Pops for Champagne and get a bottle?"

"Are you serious?" Paige asks, eyeing the beer in my hand, from which I'm taking large gulps with each swig.

"Sure. I'll go easy. I'll just grab a super-sized coffee before we head home."

"There's no way you're driving. Get your champagne, get your shots, get whatever you want, as long as you promise me two things."

"What?"

"First, I'm driving home. The whole way."

"And second?"

"You'll stay at the hotel where we met. I'll take you there, watch you check in, and then take a cab home. That'll be the end of the weekend."

"I can agree to that."

"Pops for Champagne it is!"

Paige thinks for a moment and asks, "Can I borrow your phone?"

"My phone?"

"The battery is dead on mine and I forgot the charger."

"No problem." I hand it to her, expecting her to call home, her daughter or her boss or some friend. No problem, I think.

She pulls a business card from her pocket and dials a number from it. "Hey Ted, this is Paige." She gets up and walks away, talking. Now it makes sense why she's willing to go out with me so late on a Sunday afternoon. Good old Ted is coming along. She comes back and says, "Okay, Pops for Champagne."

We get a table at Pops, next to the small stage where a few musicians gather to play renditions of old songs. Tonight's entertainment is provided by a group called King's Players. The sun is setting and it's cooling off outside as well as in. We sit down and I order a bottle of champagne. I don't mention anything about her phone call, but within a few minutes of getting our bottle, Ted walks in, wearing a white button up, a black jacket and black slacks. Paige and I are wearing shorts and short sleeves, and he looks mighty dressed up next to us. Ted is dressed to impress.

"You look nice," says Paige as Ted gives her a hug and a peck on the cheek, then shakes my hand, in a way that makes me feel like Paige's older brother. Our waiter brings over a third champagne flute and now it's the three of us with one bottle of champagne. And did I mention my head hurts?

"I'm just trying to keep up with you," Ted replies. And somehow his head isn't so red anymore, and his face doesn't seem as bloated as I remember, but he is still balding; there's nothing he can do about that. He looks at me and says, "Sorry about last night."

"For what?" I ask, certain that I'm not the one due apologies from last night.

"For going into my whole motivational talk. I do that all week, and sometimes, after I've had a few too many and been out in the sun too long, I fall back into that routine. Sorry if it bored you or just wasn't your thing."

"Oh, not at all, Ted. Don't worry about it. Happens to the best of us."

"Good."

And now I'm holding my champagne glass, rather than taking a sip and setting it down. Hold. Sip. Hold. Sip.

"So you're a psychiatrist or something, right?"

"Psychologist."

"That's right."

Ted reaches for his wallet and looks curiously inside. "Aww, I'm all out of business cards."

"That's all right," I say, pretty confident I never asked for one. But I do know the ritual, the business card trade, which always makes me laugh when it's two people who will never, ever, contact each other. But I dutifully pull out mine and hand it to him.

"Thanks." He studies it and finishes by saying, "I think Paige has my last one."

She pulls it out of her pocket and holds it up for proof.

Out of courtesy, I grab it and examine it. Ted Michaels. Professional Development Trainer. New Heights Unlimited. Fascinating. Just don't yawn. I place it back on the table, at the base of the glass candleholder, and nod approval.

We listen to the band for a while, and I notice Ted and Paige sneaking glances at each other, then blushing and looking away, like two kids in study hall who just passed notes that they like each other. The musicians play softly enough to be background music and allow for conversation, but there's an awkwardness in our threesome, understandably from my presence, yet I don't feel awkward at all.

When Paige excuses herself, Ted leans into me and quietly says, "She's a fantastic girl, don't you think?"

I nod.

"So much spark to her, strength, and yet a real underlying kindness."

I nod.

And that's when he looks at me concerned. "You two are just... I mean... Paige told me you two were just old friends, nothing else. I don't mean to be..."

"Oh no, no Ted. It's not like that at all."

"Whew. I didn't want to get in the middle of anything. Thanks."

And I can't help shaking the feeling that Ted is a nice guy. Always there to give encouragement and a helping hand, someone who would never go behind another person's back, even if that person is a complete stranger. Someone who approaches life with an innocent optimism.

"Although...," I say, piquing his interest, "...well, let me ask you this, Ted, what are your plans with Paige? I'm just curious."

"Well, like I said, I think she's a fantastic girl. So we're going to keep in touch. I'd like to visit her too, whether she comes here or I go down there, whatever's easiest."

The beginning of a relationship. The birth of a relationship, whatever that means. An open-ended beginning that will lead to who knows where or what. That wonderful joy of a beautiful road leading toward an open horizon, where anything is possible and your mind can only imagine thrilling possibilities, happy vignettes scrolling through your mind like the movie preview to a love story. But I know the end game. I know where that road can end, where wonderful open-ended futures cease to exist, and you have to live with the reality of the past.

I'm drunk and I'm panicking. I see alternate endings to this.

Luckily Ted is not treating me like competition, but instead like Paige's older brother who's looking out for her, and as such he's trying to impress me. As such, he'll listen to me. "So Ted, have you ever been married?"

"No."

"How come?"

"I was close, once. I dated a girl for eight years, but she never wanted to get married. In the end, I finally put down an ultimatum and she left. So that accounts for a good part of my years being single. Or I guess I wasn't single, but I mean I wasn't married."

"I know what you mean, Ted."

"Otherwise I've dated but it just hasn't worked out. I've been told I'm a walking example of nice guys finish last."

"Ted, that's not always true."

"That's what I'm hoping."

"Of course, Ted."

Ted, Ted, Ted. Just keeping repeating his name; let him know I'm talking to him directly. That I'm his friend. That I'm your friend, Ted. But I'm still panicking, worse than any vertigo or drunken fit, because this is real, this is the start of something, this is how it starts.

I smile sympathetically at him. I ask him, "You do know about Paige's past?" Ted freezes for a moment, but then Paige, who I had seen walking toward our table, pulls out her chair and sits down, ending our conversation about her, leaving a big question mark floating through Ted's thoughts.

Paige and Ted talk some more, close, hunched over the table, leaning into the centerpiece. I'm sitting way back, just listening to the music, taking quick deep gulps of champagne and trying to disguise them as sips, refilling my glass when no one is looking. Ted finally excuses himself, and I have a moment alone with Paige. I'm the school gossip, digging for information. The mediator. The confidant. The controller.

"So..."

"Yeah?"

"You and Ted."

"What about it?"

Paige doesn't want to give up anything voluntarily, so I have to ask directly. "What do you like about him?"

"I think I already told you."

"You did?"

"Yes. He's a nice guy. He's interested in me. He's sincere. He's fun. He's... he's nice."

"I hear nice guys finish last."

"And I know why. I've rejected them. But it was my fault, not theirs. I think I'm old enough to appreciate a nice guy."

"Good. I'm glad for you."

"Thank you."

And I still feel like her father, like I care for her well-being, but there's a separation between us, a separation of life experiences that she is too young to understand. I know things she doesn't, things I can't tell her because they are things one learns only through experience. And I feel a horrible pit in my stomach just knowing that she is going to have to learn them someday.

"If you really feel that way."

"What does that mean?" Paige doesn't finish with the word 'asshole,' but I can hear it. I wish she knew I actually care for her. I want what's best, even if we have different concepts of what's best.

"I'm just saying, it's easy to tell yourself you should like the nice guy, that it's the right thing to do. The mind can say the right things, know what's right, but the heart wants what it wants." I'm quoting Emily Dickinson, but in my mind I can hear the Beastie Boys' "Sabotage" starting up. "Listen all of y'all, it's a sabotage..."

"Why would you say that?"

"Nice guys don't finish last because girls don't think they should date them. It's because their hearts won't let them."

"Well, not only has my mind gotten wiser, so has my heart."

"So you have a good feeling about Ted?"

139

"I've only known him for a day, so who knows."

"But you have a good feeling?"

"Yes. A very good feeling."

I have a brief moment of nausea, much like when I first arrived in Chicago. My head spins for a moment and I clutch the bottom of my seat for balance. Paige doesn't notice because she's keeping her eyes on the band, and when Ted comes back, she keeps her eyes on him. I recover quickly enough, but the memory lingers. A slight nausea persists while I watch Ted and Paige flirt in the shadows of our table's flickering candle.

I'm trying to picture these two getting along. If they'll talk on the phone every night, if they'll try to meet on weekends, with Ted driving down to Paige's and occasionally Paige making her way up to Chicago. I wonder if Paige really will appreciate a nice guy, come to appreciate his enthusiasm and over-excited personality. How long will they date? Will they get married? Will they try to have kids? What happens after that?

I don't see any of that though. I see Ted's sunburned head developing stage 4 cancer. I see Paige wearing headphones, hurriedly crossing the street and forgetting to look both ways. I see Ted shoveling the driveway, oblivious to the patch of black ice. I see Paige out for a morning walk, the sun highlighting the autumn foliage, when a marble-sized blood clot loosens and begins to travel. Paige takes a deep breath but doesn't feel like she's getting any air. She drops to a knee. This is what I see. This is their ever after. I also see the small possibility of them having children. I doubt it, but it's possible, and that opens the door to all sorts of other endings I don't want to see.

And even though I was finally done drinking, I circle my finger in the air for a second bottle, and just watch them talk and flirt and laugh together, completely oblivious to me sitting there. I have to use the restroom, but hold it. Too much happens when you go to the bathroom. Too much can go wrong. I stay put and concentrate on my bloated bladder instead of playing out possible Paige-and-Ted futures.

The King's Players have gone into a string of slow songs, and two other couples who are truly on dates together have gotten up and start dancing to the right of the stage. Paige and Ted get up and join them. They move slowly, one hand around each other and one out to the side, interlocked as they spin. Paige places her face against his shoulder and closes her eyes, while Ted tries to look at the room around him but can't stop diverting his eyes down to Paige. He even breathes slowly, smelling the aroma rising from her hair and the back of her neck.

At one point he looks over at me, watching, and I raise my glass and give a nod. His face turns bright red as his teeth show a smile he just can't hold back. Ted's a nice guy and Paige is falling for him.

If she had fallen for me, things would have been better. Easier. I already know there are no long-term possibilities for us, that this was just one weekend and we would never see each other again. I would have let Paige down easily. She would move on and eventually forget this weekend entirely. But with Ted, neither one of them grasps this is only meant to be one weekend, a slip in time, a slip away from time. No long term commitments, and yet they seem perfectly willing to break the rules.

When they turn enough that neither is facing me, I reach out for the business card on the table, Ted's card that he gave to Paige, and put it in my pocket. I am fully conniving now. Listen all y'all, it's a sabotage. Our waitress comes by and I ask for a pen and paper.

Eventually the band livens up, rolling into a song paced by steel whiskers on a snare drum, forcing all the couples dancing to look at each other for a moment before heading back to their respective tables. Except Paige heads towards the bathroom and Ted comes back to our table alone, still smiling.

"We need to discuss something, Ted."

"What is it?" He's worried. He knows when things are going really well, change, any change whatsoever, is usually for the worse.

"Not here. Let's go outside."

"What about Paige?"

"She'll be all right. Here," I say, as I slide a piece of paper next to her glass. On it I have printed *Ted and I will be right back. Order another bottle.*

He gets up and starts, and I quickly reach into Paige's purse and grab her wallet and phone. She said the phone's dead, but I'm not taking any chances. We go outside quietly, and I see the wrinkles gather on Ted's reddened forehead. I lead him halfway up the block, putting ourselves out of earshot of the valet leaning against the wall, smoking. "So what do you know about Paige and me?"

"I thought you just said there was nothing between you two."

"But what do you know about us?"

"That you're two friends, visiting the city for the weekend."

"And what do you know about me?"

"Not much. You're Paige's friend."

"Mmm-Hmm."

"What's going on here?"

"And what do I do?"

"You're a psychologist."

I pause, letting him think about that. "I'm really sorry about this Ted. I shouldn't have let it get this far. I wouldn't have, but after I lost both of you last night... And tonight, I had no idea you were going to show up here, that this thing was continuing."

"Paige called me from your phone. That's what the caller ID said."

"She used my phone?" I shake my head in disgust. "I'm really sorry."

"What's going on?"

"We're not just friends," I say, and then pause. This is the point of no return. Two cars pass us on the street, a black Mercedes and a new Volkswagen bug. Three guys are walking across the street away from us, down at the corner. Two of them are laughing while the third punches one on the shoulder. A breeze picks up and the debris in the gutter rustles. "Paige is a patient of mine."

"What?"

"She's been a patient at my hospital for almost six months now. And this isn't her first visit."

"What's wrong with her?"

"You know, Ted, I'm not supposed to discuss it, I really can't." I stammer, look around, look him in the eye, and continue, "There are some things I probably can say, due to the situation. There's depression, to start with. Other issues too, but most importantly, she suffers from delusions, erotomanic delusions." That's not the correct diagnosis, but Ted only hears 'big-word' followed by 'delusions,' which is enough.

"What does that mean?"

"That means she probably hasn't told you the truth about herself. You probably have no idea who she is, her history, even her personality."

Ted steps back, holding his hands against his sides, then folding them, then holding the back of his neck, then back to his sides. He's been hit hard.

"So what do I do?"

"What should you do?"

"Yes."

"Honestly?"

"Yes, dammit."

"Get in a cab and go home."

"What? Shouldn't I talk to her, tell her I know?"

"I can handle that."

"But..."

"Look Ted, she's been playing with you, lying to you. It hasn't been on purpose, at least not meant to hurt you, but it's a problem and she knows it. It's better if I, her doctor, confront her. As long as you're there she'll try to keep the charade alive. I've seen it before, and it's not a pretty sight. And it's not good for her, intellectually or emotionally, if she's blatantly confronted by someone in her delusional state."

"What about..." Ted starts, still thinking. He doesn't want to let go. "I mean, can I talk to her at some point, show her support somehow? She could use that, couldn't she?"

"You know, I feel awful about this, Ted, I really do." I put my hand on his shoulder and look him in the eye. "Ted, she already has a support base.

She," and I pause, pretending the next lie is difficult. "This is so hard to say, but the honest truth is that she's married. She has a husband who is doing everything he can to try and help her. She has two kids, one in elementary school and one in junior high, both wondering when their mom is coming home. She has friends and relatives who would do anything for her."

"God."

"I know, and I'm so sorry."

"But why did she come up here? I mean why is she…"

"Because at the hospital, everyone knows her, knows her problems and knows her history. She can't foster her delusional worlds if no one believes her. But out here… we wanted to see how she would do with a little freedom. She clearly isn't ready. Personally, I feel like a failure. This is my fault. We haven't made nearly the progress I had hoped for, and I'm so sorry that you're caught in the crosshairs."

Ted doesn't know what to say. I tell him I'm sorry one more time, and then hail a cab while he stands in bewilderment. I shake his hand, saying, "This is for the best. If she calls, if she tries to contact you in any way, please don't respond. We need to end this and start over." He remains speechless as I help him into the cab. He doesn't say anything so I nudge him and point to the driver. He mutters an address, Old Town I think, and I shut the door, knock twice on the cab roof, and he's off, heading south on Sheffield.

My feet no longer hurt, or to be more exact, I don't feel any pain, and I jog a few blocks, zigzagging as I go, putting distance between me and Paige. I chuck her phone and wallet into some bushes along the way. I see the white barns in the room, I see where they lead, and I give myself something else to rely on. I give myself a goal. I hail a cab back to the hotel, as I have a box to bury.

BURIAL

I pick up the car in the hotel garage, as always conscious of the trapped fumes. I'm drunk and shouldn't be driving, but it's just a short distance. Not an excuse, but it is what it is, and when you're drunk these types of excuses seem to justify themselves. Still parked, I roll down the windows and rev the engine, long and hard, and just inhale, filling my lungs with carbon monoxide, and just hold it in. I can taste the gas burning, smell the oil, but I know the carbon monoxide has no taste, no smell and yet is the one that kills. I wonder about Margaret's last moments. This isn't the same though, not even close. The acrid taste and burning sensation in the lungs may be comparable, but understanding it's your last moment in the world, wondering if you might see your daughter or might never think of her, or anything, ever again, makes all the difference in the world. I'm left bleary-eyed and feeling stupid. So I put the car in drive and pull out of the parking spot, making my way out of the depths of the garage and into the city streets, heading north toward Armitage, and then west to Milwaukee. From there I drive in expanding circles, slowly maneuvering the side streets of Bucktown while searching for my destination. When I turn onto Wood Street, I see an open park followed by a church, St. Teresa Avila Church. I can't see the front, but I can see the top protruding into the night air, a large dome with a circle and a cross on top. This is what I saw from Bill and Karen's rooftop deck and the place that I chose, for whatever reason, to be my destination.

I park along the quiet streets, get out and look around. The moon hangs just above the tree line, half covered in clouds. I walk halfway into the park, surveying what's going on, if lovers are making out or maybe a drug deal is taking place. Either way I don't want to be seen, especially since I look suspicious. Not because of the Target Box in my left hand, but because of the shovel I pulled from the jack compartment. It's a miniature shovel, but a shovel nonetheless.

I walk around the stone wall that surrounds the church and into the courtyard. Inside I can't see anything but blacktop and sidewalks. Built on the urban jungle, there is no place to dig. I walk around, and along a side entrance there is a small cutout in the concrete where a row of bushes grow. This will have to do. I want to dig deep enough and am well hidden, so as not to be the man seen digging in the middle of the night. That doesn't go over well, as I know from my first Chicago return weekend.

As I survey the bushes, a loud ringing breaks out, shattering the night's sunken silence. After a moment, I realize the ring is coming from me, and I fish my phone out of my pocket and start turning down the volume, staring at the letters on the green LCD screen. "Pops Chmpgn." Paige. She must be using the bar phone. And since Ted's number is on a business card in my pocket, she's stuck calling me. She must have memorized my number, or written it down somewhere else. Regardless, I just stare at the screen, picturing her with a phone cradled against her chin, the cord draped across the bar while the bartender watches, and I watch the screen, imagine the foreboding sense of loss and anger as each ring passes without an answer, and then the LCD turns off. We are done.

I choose a spot behind the bushes, at the base of the brick wall, and jam my foot into the shovel and break ground. And just like every movie where they dig for buried treasure, where they dig to bury the bodies, where they dig to either commence or end the secret pact with earth, the familiar sound of a shovel slicing into the ground and pitching a pile of dirt begins and continues. I watch the digging as if someone else were doing the work, and dig a hole nearly two feet deep. My phone, now on vibrate, goes off a few more times, but I don't pay attention, don't count the vibrations, and don't care.

I lift the Target Box with two hands and stare at it, uncertain what to think. The locked keyhole stares back at me, wondering why I won't open it, wondering how we both got here. I set it down into the hole and proceed to scoop dirt onto it, dirtying my own hands until it is covered. I use the shovel to fill the hole and then place the carpet of grass-woven dirt on top, doing my best to hide any evidence.

I stand and stare, trying to take a mental picture that will last a lifetime, knowing that's just not possible. With an uneven mix of acceptance and denial, I turn away, with tears in my eyes and that horrible pain that feels like a shotgun blast to the heart.

I emerge from the church courtyard and try to act inconspicuous. Hoping no one is watching, I drop the shovel on the parkway, further up the block. I then get in the Mustang and drive a few more blocks, find a parking space alongside the curb, crawl into the back and sleep.

MY FATHER WAS A MINISTER AND MY MOTHER WAS A PHYSICS PROFESSOR

My father believed in Adam while my mother believed in Atom. That's how I started this story. The basic fact is my father believed there was a God watching over us, caring for us, protecting us. He believed we were created in this all-powerful being's image and are truly loved by him. My mother believed we were controlled by chance. Electrons and protons and neutrons spinning, attracting and repelling, forming an ever-increasing complexity of structures, one upon another until we humans evolved and thought and loved, societies built upon the foundation of chance.

As for me, I was never asked. It wasn't that I was taught two different viewpoints and given a choice; it was that two viewpoints co-existed, and as long as I didn't question them it didn't matter what I thought. My father's sermons were clear, as I sat in a pew near the front and listened to his interpretations of the Bible, but I also knew it was his job. He didn't preach at home unless we had visitors, and the prayers before eating, the little rituals, were as habitual and reflexive as a sneeze's "God bless you."

My mother was less overt of an influence; she wouldn't pontificate on scientific discoveries or argue with my father, but her beliefs were always there, expressed with a patronizing nod, an acknowledging *Yes*, that meant we would agree to disagree and it was time to move on.

More often than not they were not arbiters of these beliefs, but instead they were just parents. They took me to soccer practice, checked my homework, and asked how school was going. They both read a lot, my father in his den and mother in the living room, while I went out with my friends, or stayed home and watched TV. The one thing they enjoyed together were old movies, black-and-whites from eras that seemed a million years ago to a high school kid. I distinctly remember when we got Turner Classic Movies (they never called it TCM), and they spent months watching multiple movies over the weekends, planning their schedules around each weekend's lineup, filling VHS cassettes with their favorites. Old, simple, happy musicals were always their favorite. As a psychologist, I should have an opinion on that, but I have no idea why.

I'm not really sure what I believed in growing up. I understood both sides and mentally I hedged my bets by never making a decision. They both had good points and that was fine. Rather than choose a side, I chose my own way, and that was by choosing people. I believed in people. I don't say that as a rallying cry, that we can do anything we put our minds to or any of that bullshit. I just mean I believe in our existence. I know, that's not exactly a bold stance, but it's too often taken for granted. We laugh, we cry. We dance, sing, love, hate, mourn and celebrate. These feelings, these states of being that make up life are a huge expanse of motives and emotions that are real and true and amazing. But not only can I not explain anything beyond that, I never cared to.

If my father was right, if Adam and Eve ate an apple in the garden of Eden and our faith brings us salvation, then why would he create a world where processed mystery meat can choke the life from a little girl, where a few minutes without air can end the massive potential for love and joy contained within Evelyn? I heard my father's sermons about loss, remember the marquee out front for his special service, "Why does God allow bad things to happen?" But it never made sense. It never truly answered the question; it just said to suck it up and have faith. He never sat me down and told me the answer. As a father, he never prepared me for what could happen. So if my father was right, then fuck God. Fuck the Father, fuck the Son and fuck the Holy Spirit.

And if my mother was right, if Evelyn were just a collection of molecules randomly bound together to make the silken hair that rest on my cheek, to make her fingers clutch around my neck as her excited breath called out, "Daddy," if those are just stops along the survival of the fittest, if they were the same as the giraffe's long neck, the shark's sharp teeth or the cheetah's speed, then fuck evolution. Fuck that combination of protons, electrons and neutrons, fuck that strand of DNA, which makes such wonderful things as joy and love, and yet fall apart to nothing by something so unremarkably stupid as a lump of uncut hot dog.

When I look at the world and am asked to choose between there being a God or there not being a God, I have to choose neither. I believe in a small unopened wooden box that I can hold in my hands. I truly don't understand how anyone believes in anything more.

Ryan Scoville

THE TARGET BOX

There is no common way to lose a child. Living now, in the developed world, it is thankfully rare, but it still happens. It starts with those who lose a child in the womb, whether or not they have made announcements or started choosing names. Then there are those parents who make it through the whole nine month ordeal only to lose their child at the end. There are the complications during birth, followed by the hidden affliction that flares up over the next few hours, days or weeks. Usually, after that, the odds get much better, but tragedies still happen. Until the day you die, there is no guarantee you will outlive your child. Childhood cancers, brain tumors, just laying-them-to-sleep-and-never-fucking-waking-up events. There are car accidents, falls down the stairs and slips into unsupervised pools. There are abductions, stray bullets, and all sorts of crazy shit. Then as they grow older, there are the drunk-driving head on collisions, the overdoses, the joining the Army and coming back in a coffin, and the leaps off of bridges for reasons nobody comprehends. There is always a new way to lose your child.

And with what I'm about to say, I don't want to disparage anyone who has gone through that. I'm not trying to compare griefs. The lows are all the same, no matter what level of hell, they are hell. But when you're not at your lowest, when you're trying to live your life, most parents who have lost a child have also gained a cause. They have a fight. I remember watching the news, an interview with a parent whose child had been abducted and found murdered in an open field. "I will spend the rest of my life," the father said, "finding whomever committed this horrible, horrible crime, and making sure no other family ever has to go through this." Again, I don't mean to compare grief, but that man had a cause.

The March of Dimes is working to prevent preterm births by funding research as well as providing prenatal care. Mothers Against Drunk Drivers helped increase the penalties for a DUI, and probably more importantly, helped increase the stigma against drunk driving. (I know, I just drove drunk. May the good fight continue...) St. Baldrick's is fighting childhood cancer. There are those promoting peace, asking why we ever send our children off to war. There are those fighting for clean water in impoverished lands, those trying to end famine. There are fundraisers, charity drives and banquets. There are charity 5ks and half marathons and three day walk-a-thons. These are all worthwhile causes and I wish them all complete and total success.

But Evelyn choked on a hot dog. Pre-cooked pork and beef trimmings that are ground into a meat batter and then pressed into an animal intestine. From the most disgusting collection of mystery animal parts to the 100% organic, non-GMO, no antibiotic, no hormone pure beef hot dog, it's all just food. Food we eat and are lucky to eat. Where is my campaign? What is my cause? Where do I send my check? What 5K fun run should I sign up for? What charity's board of directors should I contact and say I want to dedicate my life to ending the scourge of improperly cut hot dogs?

Let's pretend all of these causes were successful, that there were no more complications at birth, no more childhood cancers, no uncovered pools, no drunk drivers and no car collisions, no famine, no disease and no war. If all these things were solved the world would be so much better. But there would still be those freak events that don't make any sense whatsoever. If the odds were one-in-a-million, one-in-a-billion, one-in-whatever, that a child would die, it would be such a better world for everyone else, but it would be the same incomprehensible hell for that child and for those parents. There would still be the end-of-your-world disaster where everyone else carries on, and you're left wondering why but with no cause to fight for. Sometimes you just need a cause.

Last Saturday, I woke up, ran, showered, read the paper, and then drove west to Lawrenceville. It's almost a forty-five minute trip and I drove the whole way with my windows down and the radio up. It's been two weeks since Chicago, the trip with Paige, and there's an empty spot above my mantel.

Six months after Margaret's passing I moved to Georgia. I had reached the point where I couldn't handle living in Chicago anymore. Too many things reminded me of the past. I didn't trust myself. My anger and resentment and grief seemed to only be getting worse with every minute spent in our house, driving down streets we used to walk along, passing the restaurants we used to eat in, seeing children swinging at the parks where Evelyn used to play. I didn't trust myself. I became resentful of my friends. I hated people on the street. I hated my patients, blathering on about problems that no longer seemed important to me.

So I moved away from it all. Moved to a place where everything was different and new. I moved to a place where I could spend my nights and weekends completely by myself and not hurt anyone. I did better with my patients, making friends only so far as a doctor-patient relationship can bear out and nothing more. I built my shelter, protecting myself from the outside and protecting the outside from me.

But I still had urges to go back. I missed Chicago. I missed my friends. I missed the restaurants and the baseball games and the bars and the plays. I missed walking the streets amidst the crowds. So I allowed myself to go back once a year. I'm not sure how it occurred the first time, where I got the idea, but now I'm walking through the parking lot, passing mothers and their children as they push bright red shopping carts full of clothes, cleaning supplies, CDs, video games, and almost anything else under the sun, and I enter the store with purpose.

There's a Wal-Mart near my house, and it would probably have what I'm looking for, but for marketing purposes I just can't go there. There's also a Target in Athens, a little further out, but I shop at that one now and then. Today I've chosen to drive out to Lawrenceville, to a Target store I only go to once a year, and as far as I'm concerned, only exists for one purpose.

I remember the first Target Box. Evelyn wasn't quite two, strapped into her seat at the front of the red cart. Margaret and I were looking at something, a picture frame, a vase, a decorative pillow, I don't remember what, but when we looked back Evie was holding it in her hands, laughing as she tried to open it but couldn't quite figure out the latch. Margaret and I looked at each other, confident we had parked Evie far enough away from the shelves of boxes that she couldn't get into trouble, yet there was the box in her hands. "No, no, Evie," Margaret said, as she tried to gently ply it from Evelyn's hands. She pulled a small stuffed elephant from her purse to distract Evelyn, but Evelyn wasn't letting go. When Margaret used a little more strength to take the box away and put it back on the shelf, Evelyn screamed.

Margaret and I looked at each other wide-eyed, surprised at the intensity of her cry, the wild scream that pierced our simple Saturday afternoon shopping trip. I'm not sure who did it, but the box was back in Evie's hands almost immediately. I know a good parent shouldn't give in so quickly, but Evelyn did not normally throw a fit like that. I can't think of another time she did that. So for $14.99 the box, which was lacquered white with daisies and violets blossoming up the sides and swirling across the sides, was hers.

Evelyn played with it all the time. She was constantly putting her favorite My Little Ponies into it, Webkinz, and plastic fruit from her plastic kitchen. I don't remember actually looking inside myself, although I'm sure I did, but I do remember it always being part of her play. She brought it with us to Disney World, but luckily left it in the hotel. It was in the car for our weekend trip to Saugatuck. And Margaret fueled Evelyn's enjoyment that it was something special. She'd ask, "What's in your Target Box, Evie?" "Are you going to put that in your Target Box?"

After Evelyn passed, I didn't think much about it. Her room was full of Evie's things, mementos and memories that could suffocate, cause an

instant panic attack just upon entering. Margaret went in that room all the
time. I never went in. And even when I found Margaret's body slumped to
the side in her Mustang, I didn't quite grasp that Evelen's Target Box was
sitting in her lap. I saw it, but Margaret was dead, and though out of place,
the box seemed such a small detail I hardly took notice. It wasn't until the
police officer handed it back to me, after the investigation, did I fully
remember that Margaret held it when she died. Back home, I couldn't bring
myself to put it back in Evelyn's room, so I placed it on the mantel.

The box followed me to Georgia. Most of Evie's stuff went into boxes,
and I hand-picked some of Margaret's stuff, her camera, special jewelry,
clothes, pictures, yearbooks, and other mementos. It's all in a storage locker
in the suburbs of Chicago. I pay annually, unsure if I will ever open it,
unsure if I ever could. But the Target Box made it to my mantel in Georgia,
as I started adding photographs to the walls and my exhibit grew. I looked
at it every day, but never opened it, never knew what, if anything, was
inside. I feared it and worshipped it, until the day came when I couldn't take
it anymore.

On that Saturday morning, where my legs ached too much after a long
run, and the lawn seemed too expansive to mow, I grabbed Evelyn's Target
Box from the mantel, put it in the front seat of Margaret's Mustang, and
started off toward Chicago. I didn't pack anything, didn't have any plans. I
had to find a hardware store downtown to buy the shovel. Then in the
middle of the night, I snuck into the lawn behind our old condo on
Mohawk and buried it. I fell asleep in the back of the Mustang, and woke
up with a left arm that was still asleep and a nasty crick in my neck. It was
early Sunday morning, and I waited outside Stanley's Kitchen and Tap until
it opened at ten. I started with a Bloody Mary. My first drink in two years,
and that was the start of a two-week bender.

The original Target Box, the one held in such regard by Evelyn and
Margaret, was buried when I first arrived in Chicago. Solemn and sober.
But all of the replicas since then, the ones that have sat on my mantel,
replaced year after year, they get buried at the end of the weekend. Drunk
and disordered. Not sure why. Perhaps I prefer being incapacitated when I
bury it, unable to really understand what I'm doing or why. Although that
seems like a strange explanation, considering I think about burying the
Target Box every other day of the year.

The store layout looks different; there's now a Starbucks tucked into the
entranceway, but I know my way. I head through the racks of clothing, past
the aisles of toothpastes and deodorants, cosmetics and shampoos, and cut
through the bedding and small furniture into the home goods section,
eventually finding myself in an aisle of knick-knacks for the home, and this
is where I start looking. Little wooden stands to place in an open corner of

your house. Picture frames and mirrors. Jewelry boxes and keepsakes to put in them. I walk up and down once, until I spot the small navy box with a white line around the lid and the silver lock in front. I pick it up and the weight feels right. I spin it in my hands, knowing I could easily twist the lid and see what's inside, but knowing I can't, that opening it and looking inside would make it a simple box from Target. The tag hanging from the side reads *Target* with a red bullseye and says *Accessory Box $19.99*. But as long as I don't open it, as long as I lock it shut and never open it, then it can truly be a Target Box. The Target Box that I will bring to Chicago next year. I hold it dutifully in my hands and head to the checkout counter. A mother unloads school supplies from the cart in front of me while her kids chase each other up and down the aisle. I patiently wait my turn. When I get back to my car, I place the Target Box on the front seat and eye it one last time. We will spend a year together, looking at each other, wondering what's inside the other.

I will then take my annual trip, which follows the aerials of a stunt plane. Take control, fly high above the waters, and then stall out and flip over into a spinning free-fall. Recover, pull myself up again, then roll out sideways and make a nose-dive towards the lake. Recover. Repeat.

Recover. Repeat.

Controlled chaos. Limited disaster.

WHERE I AM

My house isn't overly large, a single story, two bedroom bungalow, probably about thirty years old, but the lot is large. With almost four acres of open land, there is a long driveway in the front, wide open sides and a vast, slightly inclined, expanse of grass in back. I live in a neighborhood for people who don't want to be in a neighborhood. A good number of the houses similar to mine were recently torn down and rebuilt into mini mansions that have become the new normal. A week after I moved in, late May when the grass was growing like crazy from spring showers, I opened the attached garage and came out with my push reel mower. No motor at all, one hundred percent powered by push, the one I found at a garage sale and had used to mow the small patch of land in our condo downtown. I spent most of that Saturday morning on the front yard and was barely half done with it. During one of my passes some yellow gleaming beast of a truck pulled up on the side of the road and rolled down the window. I set the mower down and approached the Hummer, standing tall to see its occupant.

"G'morning, neighbor. Welcome to the neighborhood," said a voice from deep inside. We exchanged names and pleasantries. I don't remember his name, never knew where he lived, and don't see that yellow Hummer anymore so not sure if he's a neighbor anymore. But I do remember when he stopped talking, surveyed my property and chuckled.

"What?" I asked.

"Is that a push mower you're using?"

I nod.

"You from the city? Never had a lawn before?"

"I've lived a few places. I've had a lawn." When Margaret, Evelyn and I moved to the suburbs of Chicago, I bought a brand new red Toro mower. It was self-propelled and easily covered our small lot in under an hour. It's in the garage behind me, but I refuse to tell the man.

"When I first moved here," he continues, "I got me one of those John Deere riding lawn mowers, with the extra wide deck and two beer holders. That sucker could do almost 10 miles an hour if the grass wasn't too high. I'd rip out my property in about an hour. I thought that thing was great."

"Sounds nice."

"But even that got to be too much. I got a service now. Better things to do on a Saturday."

I nod.

The man grins, although I can't see his eyes behind the Ray Bans. I'm not sure if he's laughing at me or not. "You'll see. But I still got that Deere in my garage, if you want to borrow it."

"Thanks for the offer, but I'm good."

"The offer stands until I sell it. It's going to take you all day to finish. Heck, I bet it takes more than a day with that little thing. Maybe not this week or next week, but when you're sick of pushing, come by and you can borrow my Deere. Heck, I'll sell it to you for a good price. She's only got half a year's use on her."

I thank him again.

"Stubborn, I see. I get it. But you'll see. You'll want to give her a whirl soon enough. Or go straight to a service. Most of us use the same one. Bunch of Mexicans are in and out before you can get your mail. Cheap too. Let me know if you want their number."

I thank him again. We eventually end our conversation and I go back to my mower, bend down and pick up the handle. It does take more than a day. My back ached that first time. It ached the second and third time too, but I got used to it. I don't have better things to do on a Saturday.

Years go by and on any given summer weekend you're likely to catch me out mowing. Mowing or running. When training for a marathon, you're supposed to do a long slow run once a week. 10 miles, 12 miles, 14 miles, working your LSR up to a near marathon distance. I mainly do just LSRs now. I like 15 miles, usually about three times a week, depending on how well my knees have recovered from the last one. But they've gotten strong. Sometimes I have to go farther to get that sore leg burn that lasts a day or two, and feels so good. I love that burn. I love that feeling of exhaustion.

So my neighbors all know me, or at least recognize me as that crazy guy out mowing or out running alongside the highway miles away from home. I'm sure they shake their heads or outright laugh at me. I would.

It happens on a Saturday, and of course I am out mowing. I have to admit I bought a new reel mower. I still have the old one, but she kept rusting up, kept getting stuck with jammed wheels when I turned for a new pass, no matter how much oil I gave her. At some point I had to be practical, and this new one rolls like butter. I am on the side yard when the car pulls up, a small blue Ford, a cute car. I don't think much about it. It lingers halfway up my driveway for a while and I barely look up as I turn the mower near the back yard and make my way back. I don't get visitors, ever, but I do get random turn arounds, people who missed what they're looking for and use my driveway to maneuver back in the other direction. I assumed this Ford is doing the same, checking directions again, making a phone call, or something like that.

I immediately stop mowing when the car door opens and Paige steps out. I drop the mower and make a straight line toward my front door, up the porch steps and into my house. She shouts something like, "You fucking coward!" The curtains on the front bay window are drawn close, they always are, and I wait with my back against the door and breathe. I look around the front room, at the pictures on my wall, and question myself. I am a man of doubt, but that is usually a strength. Doubt is my Sampson's hair, my radioactive spider bite, but when I think of Paige and our Chicago trip two months ago, I am weakened. My feet hurt from the eighteen miles I ran this morning, but it's a sharp pain from the scar on my left foot that acts up.

There's such a long wait that I wonder if she left. It's an eight hour drive from Southern Illinois to here, and I wonder if she drove it to call me a fucking coward and then head back home. Good for her if she did.

But there is an eventual knock on the door. "I know you're in there," she shouts, but she doesn't need to. I will answer the door. I am weak but I am not a fucking coward. I open the door a bit, enough to wedge my body in the crack, the same amount I do whenever anyone comes by, the UPS guy, a prophesizing missionary or a vacuum salesman. It's just me in the door and the glimpse of a bare wall behind me. I know there is nothing to see as long as I don't open the door anymore. I am positive of that.

Paige stares at me for a long time. She was aging when we first met, and she looks older now, though it's only been two months, but she also looks lovelier. She is strong. Her brown locks fall on her shoulders, a collared shirt and dress pants that look like she just got off the train downtown and is heading to her not-quite-corner office at the ad agency. I bet she wishes she was, rather than meeting some asshole who ditched her in the city with no way home, some asshole who told the guy she liked that she's married and on hiatus from the loony bin. I wonder how long it took her to dress, how many outfits she tried on, and how stupid it now seems in front of me in my khaki shorts and a sweaty t-shirt, an old pair of grass-stained running shoes that have probably been through nearly a thousand miles of running and a hundred acres of mowing.

Paige doesn't say anything but eventually hands me an envelope. It's unsealed and I pull out a note, a three page note. My name is at the top and I start to read under her piercing gaze.

I'm not sure where to start. I guess I should start by telling you that I know everything that happened that night. I know you told Ted I was your patient. I know you told him I was married. I know you told him I was "on leave" that weekend. You told him to walk away, practically run away, and never talk to me nor return my calls. You said it wouldn't be healthy for me, like he was helping me in some way.

I know you stole my phone so I had no way to call anyone. You stole my wallet too. You left me with nothing but a wad of cash that barely paid our bill, hundreds of miles from home. Worse than that, I had no idea it was coming. I sat there so long, wondering where you and Ted went, when you would be back. I searched the table to see if I misplaced my phone. I went back to the bathroom so many times. I never expected anything like that, ever. I couldn't imagine someone would do something so awful.

I've thought about that a lot and still can't figure it out. You're the psychologist and I wonder if you know. There's something wrong with you, more than just being a vicious drunk, but being a bad human being. An awful human being. You are an awful human being.

I take a deep breath and look up from the note and Paige knows exactly where I am, could probably mouth the words herself. I look back down to continue reading, but Paige reaches out and takes the note from me and I let her. I have a good idea what it says, and she'll feel better telling me.

"I spent so much time writing that note... no, no…. I didn't."

I don't budge, don't give her an expression, and just stare as if she's telling me how Jesus saves or how much dirt is in my carpet.

"I don't want you to know how this affected me, but it did. I have to be honest that it did. But I also have to be honest that it made me stronger. I got home. I won't give you the details, you fucking asshole, but I made it home. I'm in nursing school and I'm doing well, really well. Whatever your intent was, however you tried to hurt me, it only made me stronger."

I continue to stare.

"I keep trying to figure you out, and in one of those scenarios I imagine you saying, 'You're welcome', like it was some plan of yours to make me stronger. Like you knew it all along and were pulling the strings. You think you know everything. I can't imagine how horrible of a psychologist you are."

I'm actually very good, to be honest. If you asked my patients, my coworkers, my boss, they'd all say I do a great job of accomplishing exactly what a psychologist is supposed to do. It's probably because I have distance, because I'm not fully invested, that I'm good at achieving what I'm supposed to do and not impaired by what I want to do. It doesn't matter though.

"You're wrong," are the first words I speak to Paige.

She stares at me and waits. I see a flash of worry that I'm going to take this confrontation some direction she didn't expect, play some word jujitsu that leaves her bumbling and apologizing. She's worried because she won't let that happen, can't let that happen, and yet anticipated it the entire car ride down here.

"You were strong all along. From the first moment you left your friends and approached me I knew you were strong. If what happened made you stronger, then I apologize, as that's the last thing I wanted to do."

"What?"

"I guess I just don't believe you can be strong enough. No one can be strong enough and it's foolhardy to think otherwise. This I know. No matter how strong you are, you can't be strong enough."

Paige has questions, wants to ask them, but knows she can't. She can't follow my lead and needs to stick to her script. "When I finally realized I was alone, that you left me..."

Stop, I signal with raised palm. Instead, I pull open the door and step back. "Come inside," I say, "just for a moment." As I step back, Paige sees the first column of canvas pictures on the wall, the ones I normally hide from view with my body. She steps into the entryway, and though the curtains are pulled, the sun still shines through, and I turn the lights on full. It's not enough though, and I go through the trouble of opening the front bay curtains, curtains that I have never opened since moving in, and let sunlight fill the house.

Margaret backed up all her pictures on a hard drive. After she died I backed that up three more times, one for my own safety, another for a safe deposit box, and a third to give away. There were over one hundred thousand pictures. Not all were of Evelyn. Some were from photo shoots, where she could rip off a hundred shots or more pretty easily. But there were so many of us. So, so many.

I never looked through them all though. Instead, I took that third backup hard drive and gave it to Margaret's photographer friend Beth at Margaret's funeral. I took her aside and gave her very clear instructions. I told her I had a spot over our fireplace that had a family picture. I asked her to take a picture from the hard drive, any picture that had Evelyn or Margaret in it, create a canvas and send it to me. I asked her to keep doing it, a new one once a month, that I could rotate over the fireplace. I would pay her for each one, pay her more than the going rate, and she would keep doing it as long as I asked. It was steady income for a photographer, which was always welcome, but I knew it would be hard to look through the pictures of a dead woman and her dead child and make happy portraits; I knew it would be hard to photoshop ghosts. Beth asked me if she thought it was wise, if it would be good to be reminded every month, but with my wife lying in an open casket in the next room, she agreed to whatever I asked.

At the end of each year she always emailed me and asked if she should continue. I always said yes. After two years she told me she couldn't continue, didn't like revisiting Margaret's photos every month, and asked if she could get someone else, someone whose work she really respected, to continue. Someone who didn't know Margaret at all. I agreed, and asked the new photographer to start sending me two a month. I pay $300 per picture, and it's the most important investment I make. It's been almost 8 years, and I have nearly 800 unique portraits.

They're not all the same size, but the majority are 20"x 24" inches. I can fit about 40 of these on the main wall in the front room, across from the bay window, if I go floor to ceiling, with a two inches between. That's my largest wall and every square inch is used. Actually, every square inch of the front room is used, with about 60 pictures overall.

Evelyn just old enough to sit up, in a white dress, perched in a field of yellow lilies. She is picking at a clutch of wildflowers, the petals falling in her lap. Three pictures, a black and white montage, from the hospital room after Evelyn was born. One of me nervously holding her by the hospital room window, one of her being weighed and measured beneath the heat lamp, and in the middle a picture of Margaret in bed, looking worn and tired from six hours of labor, but with a sparkle in her eye as she looks down on the sweet pea cradled in her arms. Nearby is our first Cubs game, Evelyn on my shoulders beneath the Wrigley sign, grasping my hands above the crowd of revelers. There's an old barn, painted bright blue, out somewhere past the western suburbs that Margaret loved to visit. Not only was it painted a beautiful iris blue framed in white, but as Margaret said, "It had character." There's a picture of Evelyn in a floral dress, standing inside the barn's half-open front door. There's one of her up the drive from it, the entire barn out of focus in the distance, like an impressionist painting. There's one of Evelyn's white shoes, discarded on a blue blanket at the base of the barn. On the other side of the room is one of Evie lying next to them, her dress spotted in mud with disheveled locks of hair curling across her forehead. I think Margaret had a shoot that day, the first photos always of Evelyn before the customer arrived, and the latter ones at the end of the day after Evie played all day. There's Evelyn in a high chair outside O'Brien's restaurant on Wells, holding up a spoon and showing the beginnings of a toothy smile.

Pictures follow down the hall, into the second bedroom, which is also full. With fewer windows, and with the closet doors removed to make more wall space, I've managed to hang almost 70 pictures.

Of course there are holiday pictures. Evelyn in her bouncy chair beneath a Christmas tree. Evie in white, with purple bows and curled lace, dragging an Easter basket behind her, bright plastic eggs spread across the lawn. Evelyn the lamb, our lamb, with a Halloween bucket at her side, looking up at the neighbor's door, about to knock. Evelyn's face laughing in delight, before the glow of a sparkler. Evelyn covered in chocolate cake, having mixed it into a paste across the surface of her high chair, a Happy 1st Birthday hat protruding sideways from her head.

The iconic one of the three of us before the Disney castle, the blurred silhouette of Cinderella not too far to the side. Evelyn in a pink and blue swimsuit, clapping on a water pad as sprayed droplets of water take flight overhead. In the stroller on the pathway up to Lincoln Park Zoo. A beautiful close up of Evelyn laughing, presumably right after crying, as there are tear marks down her ruddy cheeks and a glossy sparkle in her eyes. Her mouth is unmistakably open with a laugh, her perfect baby teeth exposed, her little tongue pressed to the side. I don't know why she was crying. I don't know why she was laughing. But I do remember Margaret showing me that picture, bringing it up on the back of her camera, both of us finding amazement in what we had created, what had been bestowed upon us. So many photos of amazement.

The front bathroom has almost twenty. I never use the shower in there, and ended up putting nails through the grout to hang more. Pictures line the space between the windows and ceiling. Pictures are propped against the fireplace stone. Pictures hang in the closets, from which I've removed more doors.

The back bedroom is close to three-fourths full. The walls look covered, but I know I can take them all down, plan a new layout, and get quite a few more on the wall. I've done this in the other rooms, spending a weekend taking them down and laying them across the floor, measuring, drawing and rearranging until I get the layout I want. I've asked for smaller prints too, 16"x 20"s and even 8"x10"s, mainly so I can fill gaps here and there. I should easily get a few more years in this house, but not sure what I'll do once there is no more room on the walls. I've thought about putting up some accordion partitions in the front room, like in a museum, and that will buy some time. I have so little furniture it would be easy to do. I could move, but would prefer staying here. This house fits my needs well. It has so many memories hanging on its walls, it just doesn't seem right to move. I've thought about contracting an addition, a back room with one doorway in, no windows, but plenty of skylights. I like that idea the most.

I don't show Paige the back rooms, but she can see the pictures running down the hallway. She can pretty easily assume they're everywhere.

"They are...?" Paige asks.

"My wife, Margaret, and our daughter Evelyn."

"They are...?" Paige asks, knowing already.

"Dead."

I know Paige is horrified, but I'm not sure if she's horrified for me or of me. This isn't normal, of course, but it should be. I counsel people who've lost loved ones all the time, and they're right that time is what heals all wounds. It doesn't really heal though, it just builds distance in the mind. You forget the sound of their voice, the funny things they used to say, the feel of their hand in yours, and the sparkle in their eyes. I'm doing everything I can to shorten that distance.

"How are you a psychologist?" Paige asks.

"I'm a good one, a really good one, at least as far as what a psychologist is supposed to do. I help people the way they want to be helped. They work through their issues, I help them move on and make their lives better. I tell them it will work out in the end. I do everything I learned to get my degree and I do it well, just like the textbooks prescribe. But I feel like I'm fixing sails while ignoring the hurricanes on the horizon. There are things you just can't escape no matter how hard you try. It feels like I'm only fixing people enough for them to break again.

"I do my best all year, but it builds up until I can't take it anymore. I can't be the good doctor. I need to stop lying for once. I need to scream and punch and be a wild animal just for a moment, and I need to stop helping people try. I need to do the opposite."

Paige wants me to say I'm sorry. I'm sure of that. I think if I say those two words, she'll look around the room once more, at the hundreds of portraits, magnified and cropped and smoothed and sharpened, this intense wall of lost perfection, and then leave. But I won't. I'm not completely sure why I did what I did, but I'm not sorry for anything anymore. I'm sorry for the world we live in, and what I do is just insignificance in the storm.

We stand there a while longer, Paige looking back and forth between the many pictures and me. "I'm going to go now," she finally says.

There once was a connection between us, I think. "All right."

She starts towards the door, the knob in her hand, and asks, "What was in the box, the Target Box?"

I don't know, I first think. I really don't. I never opened it. I want to tell her something profound, like the answers are in the box, but know that doesn't mean anything. I could tell her my heart is in it, my soul. Everything and nothing. The beginning and the end. All of them sound stupid. "I don't know," I answer, "probably nothing, perhaps everything," I say, realizing it always sounds stupid, "I just don't know."

"What did you do with it?" she asks, staring at her hand wrapped around the doorknob.

"I buried it."

"Is that what you were supposed to do with it?"

I gaze at all the pictures staring back at me and ponder what exactly I was supposed to do with the Target Box, what I am supposed to do going forward. This conversation is going nowhere. "Goodbye, Paige," I say.

She pauses for a thought but says nothing, and instead exits, closing the door with purpose.

I listen as Paige gets into her car and drives away. I don't feel like mowing anymore, so I go out to the garage and get into the Mustang. As always, the key is in the ignition. I turn it on and the tape deck plays "The Best of OMD," a tape I bought for Margaret on Ebay and planned to give her for Christmas. I actually enjoy their synth/pop now, but turn off the stereo and rev the motor. I inhale as the engine shakes and roars. I grasp the steering wheel and close my eyes, swallowing the wretched air.

Along with the tears comes something that feels like determination, but there's just not enough and I eventually get out. I always do. I get out and lift the garage door, releasing the Mustang's choking exhaust into the crisp fall air. I pull the car out, turn it off, and get out a bucket and soap. I never drive the Mustang. Once a month I pull her out, rev the engine, wash her down, and put her back in the garage. The water is cold and my hands tingle as I sponge soap across the hard top. It's fall, and the sun is about to set, but I need another run today, a long one, an exhausting one. When I'm done washing the car I will change into my running clothes. I will dress warm, long sleeves, gloves and a hat, and trudge out into the darkness.

Ryan Scoville

ABOUT THE AUTHOR

This is Ryan Scoville's second novel, following *The Slithy Toves*. He currently resides in Illinois with his wife, three children, a Newfoundland and a Bernese Mountain Dog. Lots of love and lots of hair.

Made in the USA
Monee, IL
23 April 2021